The Community

BRYAN PETITT

For my son and daughter. Without them, the motivation to attempt great things would not exist.

Be humble for you are made of earth.
Be noble for you are made of stars.
— Serbian proverb

Prologue

Los Alamos, New Mexico - 1942

"THIS is the day," the scientist says to himself as he slowly climbs out of bed. *The day I become famous. The day I change the course of history. The day I make this country even stronger.*

He gets ready for work like normal, in his usual slow and methodical way. He eats breakfast while reading the paper, checking on the status of the country he loves.

The war is getting worse every day. The fighting doesn't seem like it will ever stop, and encompasses multiple continents. More and more soldiers die, with no real means to an end.

Until now, he thinks. *I have a means to an end. If only they knew what I was going to do. They wouldn't have even brought me aboard that godforsaken ship.*

The ship's inhabitants had no idea what they were doing. The man they brought aboard in good faith has decided to use their technology not to persuade humans to change their ways, but to help destroy them.

Finishing the paper, the scientist stands and heads for the door. He grabs his briefcase on the way out and ensures everything is there and intact.

On the short drive to work, he ran over his plan. He needs to convince his partner first. The rest will come once he has someone on his side. He arrives at the laboratory, and finds the man he is looking for. He explains his idea on their way to their research area.

"This is it," the scientist told his partner as they walked through the long, bleach white hallway. Heading deeper into the depths of the research laboratory of Los Alamos, their voices get quieter as they pass unsuspecting workers.

"What do you mean, this is it?" his partner asks. "We haven't even done any research. We don't know what the yield will be, or how much plutonium we'll need. We have absolutely no proof of concept, but you expect us to just begin work based on your word?"

"Yes, that is what I expect," the scientist replies. "Trust me. This *will* work."

"Well I hate to tell you, but we are not going to do anything just because you have complete confidence in some untested theory of yours. This will go through the regular process, just like everything else has. It will be years before we can be sure anything works."

"All of this is unnecessary," the scientist says. "Just look over it. You will see. My theory is sound." *It has to be. They gave me complete access to their machines. I don't understand most of it, but I did get enough information to aid me in creating an implosion nuclear bomb.*

"I'll look over the material. But in no way does that mean we are going to use your method. I still don't see how you could have just come up with this on your own."

I didn't, he thinks. *I had plenty of help. They just didn't realize what they were giving me at the time.* "I don't really understand it either," he says. "But when the idea came to me, I ran with it. This is what I came up with. It will work. I ran the numbers over and over. All you have to figure out is the right amount of plutonium. I can assure you, this is much more efficient than the gun-type bomb you have been working on."

"We'll see," his partner replies. "We have a lot of testing to conduct before we can be sure."

"I am one-hundred percent confident that it will work," the scientist states. *I just hope I didn't sell my soul for it to be this way. The world is losing an amazing opportunity, but this is more important.*

··●··

Two weeks later, the project is under way. The director himself congratulated the scientist, though even he was unsure how to man came up with the idea and calculations so fast. But it worked, just as he said it would.

An implosion bomb. *Who would have guessed?* The scientist thinks. No one ever even considered building a nuclear bomb this way. The gun style bomb of the ideas past was the only way to go before now.

He stands there, overlooking the canyon, and considers his new position within the scientific community. People know his name. He has standing. His word is trusted. It's everything he ever dreamed of.

But he shouldn't have done it. He realizes this now, after the fact. The miracles that could have been weigh too heavily on his heart. *There would have been no need for my device at all,* he thinks. This is what would have ended all wars, not the bomb I have designed.

As the New Mexico heat warms his skin, he is filled with regret. *Everything I did, I did to better myself and my country. But to what end? I did not need to better myself or my country when such amazing possibilities were within our grasp.* The disappointment overtakes him, and he begins to sob.

I will miss the beauty of space, though, he thinks, as he looks up to the sky. He knows he will never again see the stars in the same way. *If there is another life, I'm sure the stars will be taken from me there, too.* He can't bear to think about what he is now missing out on. *What have I done?*

Peering over the edge of the canyon again, he decides there is only one thing left to do. "I won't be needing this anymore," he tells himself, pulling the metal box from his briefcase. He looks at it one last time, admiring the simple beauty of it before he throws it over the side.

With the grief and despair of his actions coursing through his veins, he takes one final look at the beautiful, clear blue sky. The tears flow faster, and he makes another life changing decision. Looking back down, he jumps, following the metal box to the bottom of the canyon.

··●··

Standing in front of the holographic computer screen, the tech shakes his head. *The psychologist isn't going to be happy about this*, he thinks. *And I know the chief scientist won't either.*

He calls them to the station, knowing what is going to happen. It's disappointing. *We had so much hope for them.*

When they arrive, he tells them what he has witnessed. They ask to see the data, and he obliges. After that, he pulls up the video feed. Watching the scientist, and listening to his past conversations, their conclusion is immediate. It is time to go home.

The actions of the scientist at Los Alamos are unforgivable. *There is no way the council would ever allow them to join now. Not after that. He has ruined their chances for another fifty years, at least. The council may even extend that because of this egregious action.*

The chief scientist and psychologist walk away, discussing how to bring this up. The council will be devastated. It is hard to watch a brink species make such a terrible move. It is even more unfortunate to see that one man is the cause of it. *And to think, we are the ones who gave him the technology he is now using to create destruction. We have a lot to learn about humans,* the tech thinks.

The only solace he finds is in the fact that the man eventually saw the error he made. While the last choice he would ever make was regrettable, it did show him that the scientist had a conscience. *How sad, though, that he only just now found it.*

With a tear in his eye, he turns his monitor off. He won't need it again until they reach their next location. *Hopefully next time, we can find someone that is actually worthy of our effort. It seems we were wrong about Earth.*

Part

1

From Knowledge Comes Freedom

Astronomy compels the soul to look upward, and leads us from this world to another.
— Plato, The Republic, 342 BCE

· 1 ·

The Article

Charlottesville, Virginia - 2016

SLAMMING my phone down, I turn back to my laptop. "Damn calculator app only goes up to 15 numbers," I grumble to myself as I start punching in the zeros on the computer. Unfortunately, I need more than that. Getting to the fifteenth zero, and then adding the one, I stare at the screen for a minute. That *is* a big ass number. One quadrillion stars in just the average supercluster, and there are at least ten million more of them. And we can't even see over ninety percent of those stars. *And I never will,* I think. Crazy. It's hard to imagine that when I look up, I'm not seeing the end. Hell, it's barely the beginning. I decide to use .0001 percent to start. Seems like a tiny enough number. A long shot, and in my opinion, one hell of a low-ball. *I did promise a low-ball, I guess.* I hit the Enter key.

I don't even know why I'm doing this, I think, as I copy and paste the result into my notes to save for later. *Writing an article about the chances of alien life. Like anyone really cares.* I might get ten people to read it. The political stuff matters. But no one really cares about space anymore. What's the point? "Screw em," I think aloud. I enjoy learning about all of this regardless.

And learn, I have. It turns out that the universe isn't just a bunch of galaxies floating around aimlessly through space. They're grouped together, just like solar systems of planets. The galaxies can orbit each other like planets orbit a star. And there are millions of them. Seriously. And each one can have hundreds of billions of stars. These galaxies group together to make superclusters. And the superclusters? There are at least ten million just in the parts of the universe we can see. Really makes you feel tiny, right? And don't even get me started on dark matter. That's a different article altogether.

I've become so interested in space lately, so addicted, that I've gotten my wife, Brynn, interested as well. She says it's my enthusiasm. Something about how much I love it, rubbing off on her. I guess she can't help but love it when I used to drag her around to observatories as often as possible. Or maybe it was the nights spent on the hill behind the house, laying on a blanket and watching the stars slowly spin by, as we make small talk and cuddle for warmth. That was also the first time I heard those three sweet words leave her lips. "I love you, Ira." she had said, as if it was the most normal thing in the world at the time, both of our eyes in the sky, our hands clasped together. Yeah, that's probably it.

One day, I'll have my kids interested too. I can't wait for the day I can show my son, Wes, the night sky through a telescope, pointing out planets and stars and all the worlds we can only see through glass. Believe me, he'll love it. *He better, dammit*. He doesn't have a choice. Hopefully, things will change and he can actually go to school and make something of himself. Do the exploring and discovering I only wish I could do. Maybe I'll hit the jackpot and get my daughter, Beth, to love it as well. As much of a handful as she is right now, she's smart. I think she could figure out the mysteries of dark matter before she figures out high school. And my other kids, Brynn's daughters from her first marriage, are trouble. Getting Lynn and Marie to pay attention is like trying to herd cats. *But I love em!* I'll teach them everything I know, regardless. *You can lead a horse to water*, I think to myself, smiling.

Continuing the calculations, I become lost in thought again. With all of the information I was able to find, there was one bit that seemed elusive. I could find so little about *intelligent* life, that I won't be able to add it to my article. I told myself that I would only use information if I were able to find it through multiple verified sources, and I won't change my mind about that. I want this article to be nothing but complete fact. Well, except for the percentages I use. There's no real way to make that fact. But there has got to be intelligent life out there as well, right? I can't imagine that we're the only ones in the universe that can think for ourselves. There's plenty of reasons they wouldn't want to visit, so that can't be an excuse to say they don't exist. If they're more intelligent than us, we'd be nothing to them. Why would they have any need to visit Earth? There are plenty of other planets where they could gather resources. If they're less intelligent, well, that explains itself. We couldn't even fathom space travel until the 1950's. Surely they can't travel in space yet if they're less intelligent than us.

Maybe we're near-equal. I laugh to myself, picturing some other *thing* typing away at a holographic computer terminal somewhere, just like me, trying to wrap its brain around extraterrestrial life. It seems silly, anyway, that no one in the science community has ever seriously hypothesized about the chance of there being intelligent life elsewhere in the universe. Or made an equation for it. "They have an equation for everything else," I say to myself.

Realistically, I know why no one questions things anymore. We're not allowed to. After the last election, a lot of changes happened very fast. No one believed the president would actually do half of the things he said. But he did, and worse. Almost immediately, new laws were passed, preventing anyone from questioning the government. Not in private, and definitely not in public. Harsh punishments are slammed down quickly if you do. Shortly after, the borders were sealed. Great walls were erected, pushed deep into the earth and high into the air, preventing anyone from crossing. No person or thing is allowed to enter or exit the country. Including information.

Once the walls were complete, the flow of information stopped. Nothing new could make its way into the country. Even the internet was restricted, with un-hackable firewalls preventing access to any websites outside of the US. More laws were enacted to keep everything closed off. No research is done without his permission. Universities can't even conduct research in the name of education, unless it meets his strict guidelines. It rarely does. All money was diverted from projects, government and private alike, and fed into the churning wheels of "progress." Things like defense and weapons spending skyrocketed, and construction on the wall, while everything else fell by the wayside. Everything is now "Made in the USA," again, but at an astronomical cost.

Once common foods are now unavailable. Even more electronics are impossible to find. Smuggling is getting worse, and the penalties are severe for being caught with something not made here. Even more so for being caught smuggling. Air pollution is slowly climbing, since more and more manufacturing companies are opening their doors, now with no laws restricting their practices. Other nations are blocked out as well, though few want anything to do with the US after all of these changes. While life has continued on the same for most people, it's scary to think what this country has become. Soon enough, everything will suffer, with no new information getting to the public.

So people now rely on folks like me. Doing my own research, making my own calculations. No funding goes into it, so it slips through the one loophole in the law. The government hates it, but they're currently powerless to do anything about it. The only thing I use is time. Early mornings, late nights. Before and after work at the plant, using any time not dedicated to the family for tying little pieces of old information together, creating links no one thought to make before. Who knows if I'm even getting it right, but at least I'm trying. I wouldn't exactly call the people like me an organized resistance. We're just men and women trying to keep the past alive, in hopes that one day it will become the future again.

Finished with the calculations, I begin my next paragraph. "So. Math again! Let's go back to that one quadrillion number..." I peck away, focused again on the task at hand. *I really need to work on my typing*, I think to myself. *What kind of person that wants to be a writer never takes a typing class?* After a few minutes of back and forth, checking my notes and typing, I finish the paragraph and lean back into the couch. *Okay, break time.* These paws need a rest.

Pulling myself off of the couch, I wander into the kitchen for a drink. *Water*, I tell myself. Healthy. Thinking back to my reason for drinking boring water instead of a delicious soda, I wonder where she is. *The girls went to their dads today*, I remember. *She had errands to run.*

Water in hand, I head to the front porch for a smoke. Good luck getting me to quit that. *Okay, only so healthy.* I grab the dog, our yellow lab/cocker spaniel mix, and attach his leash on the way. *Might as well get the lazy thing some sun while I'm out here.* I sit on the edge, resting my legs on the second step down, and enjoy the spring weather. The dog wanders off into the slowly growing grass to do his thing. "Damn, I don't wanna start mowing again," I say to myself as I shake my head. I can think of a million other ways to use that time.

Like writing. I've always loved doing it. It eases stress and helps me relax. Math problems, not so much, but when it's for my current subject, space, I don't mind a bit. I've loved space longer than I have loved writing. It's enthralled me ever since I was young. The vastness, the unknown. It's amazing and inspiring. Or I could spend time with my family, my absolute favorite thing to do. The kids are my life, and there is nothing in this world that could change that. Without a doubt, they have changed me for the better. They could never know how much they mean. And I don't know where I'd be without Brynn, the strongest and most amazing woman I know. Basically, I'd rather be doing anything but cutting the grass.

Looking at the trees, I notice they're starting to bud. Small, green tips sit at the end of each branch, just waiting for the right moment to spring open with leaves, sucking in the sunlight and water. I can't wait. Spring and summer are my favorite times of the year. The grass is getting greener every day. Flowers have begun sprouting, finally pushing through winter like the rest of us. I can hear more and more birds chirping as well. Robins, finches, blue jays, and everything in between. The woodpeckers are looking for bugs in the trees while the other birds hunt for them in the seasonally moist spring ground. Yep, spring is finally here. It scares me to think that one day, spring days like this won't be as beautiful, with the ozone being eaten away at an exponential rate, and no imported flowers to enjoy.

·· ● ··

Standing up from his station, the analyst walks over to the Captain. *I can't believe it. Finally, I think we've got someone with potential.* He walks faster, his excitement building over his decision to advocate for someone.

Reaching the Captain, he starts with no hesitation. "I think I've found the one, sir."

Surprised, the Captain whirls around to look the analyst in the eye. "How long have you been studying him before you came to this conclusion?"

"I've studied most of his life, sir. I got his background information, then began going over his actions in the past two years."

"Okay. That's a good start. Tell me about him."

"He has a family. Four children, and a wife. Two of the children aren't his biologically, but he treats them as if they are."

"Interesting," the Captain interrupts. "But continue."

"He lives in the United States. After their leader closed off the country, he immediately began doing things not many others did. He researches on his own, and posts his findings online for others to see. He disagrees with what his government does, and he walks a thin line between safety and arrest."

"What kind of research does he do?"

"Well, sir, right now it's space. He's currently using old scientific data and trying to build new conclusions from it. He's hypothesizing how many planets in the universe may have advanced life."

"Quite the coincidence, don't you think?" asks the Captain. "Tell me more."

"Well, though he doesn't seem to talk about it much, he has also served in his country's military. While we denounce war, it does show a level of dedication and commitment to a cause. He was also in a position of leadership before he left the service."

"Okay let me go get my partners," the Captain says. "You may be right. This seems like exactly what they were looking for."

He leaves to retrieve more people, and the analyst looks back to his screen. *Maybe we really can make this work.*

The Captain returns with two other people. The analyst goes over everything again, explain this new person in great detail.

"Do you have any other information?" one of the men ask.

"Yes. He doesn't litter, and doesn't appear to be wasteful. He cares about his surroundings, and is passionate about everything he does. He's trying very hard to hang on to whatever is left of his country."

The three men confer together, making 5 minutes seem like what must be hours for the analyst who is waiting. All he can hear is hushed whispers. He can see their faces, but none give away a thing.

Finally, they turn back to him. "How sure are you?" the Captain asks. "You are the one who has been studying him."

"I am positive, sir. If there is anyone that is ready, it is him."

"Well, in that case, bring him in. I'll grab a few men to prepare."

With that, the three men walk away. The analyst, a huge grin on his face, spins back to his station. His fingers fly, throwing commands to his computer as fast as he can. *I sure hope this works.*

··●··

My cigarette finished, I look down at the sidewalk to see the dog laying down in the sun already. *Figures.* I give the leash a tug. "Time to go inside, boy," I say as

I open the door. He lopes up the steps, taking his time. Apparently, going inside is an inconvenience. "I know damn well if I left you out here, you'd be whining in 5 minutes to come inside," I tell him. Ignoring me, he walks through the door. I pause on the stoop and look up at the blue sky, my mind wandering back to my article for a second, before I finally shut the door.

I unclip the leash after I close the door, and he takes off after the water bowl. *Five minutes of sun was just too much,* I suppose. He'll be passed out on the couch soon. Looking back out the window, I decide to grab a chair and my computer and write outside. I'd take coffee, but the stuff grown in the US tastes like garbage compared to the delicious coffee we used to buy. I've learned to live without it. I don't need it outside, anyway. It's my favorite place to be, and I might as well soak up the fresh air while I can. Everyone will be home soon, and then I'll be done for the day. I check the clock. *4:45. Forty-five more minutes.*

I turn from the window just in time to see the dog slide around the corner and sprint down the hall. His tail is between his legs, ears are low, and the hair on his back standing straight up. I can even hear a whine between the clack of his nails on the hardwood. *What the hell scared him?* I wonder. *He never moves that fast.* I call his name and get no response but silence. Stepping into the kitchen again, I see nothing wrong. *He'll live,* I think to myself. *Probably got water up his nose or something. He's special.*

I walk into the living room to grab my computer.

Just before I get to the couch, I pause. Something doesn't feel right. Not the horror movie kind, where people just get a 'feeling,' the real kind. *The dog must have just felt it before I could.* I can feel it in my bones, almost like a vibration. *That's it. A vibration.* "What the hell?" I ask aloud. As I walk to the window, the feeling becomes stronger. And stronger. Definitely vibrating now, I can see other things doing it as well. Pictures on the wall, trinkets on the mantle. Vibration turns to shaking. Shaking gets harder. Then things start falling. The pictures, the trinkets. Almost me. I can hear other things falling in the house now too. Boxes stored in the basement, tools from the workbench, all making their way to the floor. *Earthquake?!*

I struggle the rest of the way to the window so that I can look outside. Nothing. The birds are still flying, making lazy arcs across the sky. Cars are still driving, slowly coasting down the hill in front of the house. A gentle breeze swaying the trees, making them dance slowly in front of the puffy clouds floating through the blue beyond. Normal, everywhere, except in my stormy house. *What in the hell is this?!* I think, turning from the window.

Vibration turns to noise. Like a phone vibrating, but hundreds of times worse. My ears burn, my head is pounding, and I can barely stand. Placing one knee on the floor for support, I keep my eyes swiveling, trying to find the source.

And then comes the wind. *Wind?!* It's like a vortex, a small tornado, blowing through my house.

Whipping my hair around, stirring up and throwing the things that have already fallen, and picking up other things as well. The kids' toys, dishes, clothes that should've been folded, anything loose. Terrified, I get onto both knees and cover my head. I squeeze myself into the corner where the couch meets the wall, seeking the only protection I can find. It keeps getting louder, and I think I feel something running from my ears, down my cheeks. I open my eyes to see drops of blood on the floor, the only expected sight amid all this chaos. My body is rattling so hard, I feel as if I could rip apart. The wind feels like it is strong enough to tear the house down any minute.

And then, it stops.

Silence. Stillness. Confusion.

Sounds begin to trickle in. My heart, pounding loud enough to wake the neighbors. Dripping water, from a busted pipe or broken glass of water. The house groaning, re-settling on its foundation. The dog, whimpering, in another room down the hall somewhere. A few things finish tumbling to their final resting point.

I grasp the edge of the couch and stand, slowly regaining my footing. I look around at the nightmare that is what's left of the interior of my home. *What in the hell just happened?* I spin, looking for my phone so I can call my wife. *How do I explain this?!* I get down onto my knees again, scouring the floor. I'm frantic now, the shock of what happened finally hitting me, adrenaline wearing off.

I feel a slight vibration again, and nearly bolt out the door. I look up from the floor and see a ball of what must be electricity. Blue, silver, and powerful, slowly filling the room, little bolts like static sizzling off of it in every direction. It sounds like electricity, hissing and popping, each little bolt frying the air around it. It gets brighter and brighter, and my terror is back. Speechless, thoughtless, all I can do is stare at this growing mass of power. Time slows down, seemingly crawling by while the electricity fills the room. The hair on my arms, and surely my head, is standing straight up, everything nearby now charged by this enormous ball of energy. It's blinding now, and loud, and it takes all my energy to yank my eyes away and force them closed. Just in time to miss the flash, bright like the sun, fill the room. But I feel it. God, do I feel it.

Schzwack! The bolt hits me like a train, and my vision goes black like the night sky.

Finally, calm.

· 2 ·

Grey

Unknown Location

IWAKE up face down and flop onto my back, expecting to feel soft carpet beneath me, or the warm sunlight streaming in. Hoping to see the white ceiling above me, a window with budding trees and blue sky to my left. Waiting to hear the hum of the fridge, the snoring dog, the distant chirp of birds.

Instead, I see metal. Dark metal ceiling, barely visible through pipes and wires, conduit shuttling who knows what through the room I'm in. Metal walls with no windows, which makes me think I'm underground, or in the middle of some structure. A metal floor, filled with rivets and bolts. Grates cover holes to the unknown, one with steam slowly seeping out. Everything is a dull grey, gritty in places, as if it's had hundreds of years of use. The smell of oil reaches my nose, surely lubricating machines that serve unknown purposes. And I do hear a hum though it's definitely not the fridge. It's the hum of the distant machines, churning and firing, constantly running, sending power wherever it is needed. The lighting is dim, emanating from an obscure source, seemingly just existing in the room. I can see a door, metal again, on the wall across from me. The corners are rounded and flush with the wall. It is closed, and I can't seem to spot any type of mechanism to open it.

Cautiously, I sit up. Turning my neck to each side, I stretch the kinks out, as if I've been asleep for hours. I test my finger and toes, then legs and arms, and find that I'm not hurt. *Why am I so surprised that everything works? How long have I been here?* I wonder. And better yet, *where is here? God, I need a cigarette.*

My assumption so far is that I have been arrested for something. I know I come close, but I don't think I've ever crossed the line completely. I have spoken out about the political process, but not about the country or any particular politician. Especially not the president.

And if I have been arrested, I still have no idea what this place is. It could be some kind of prison, but it's nothing like I've ever seen before. I thought they had metal bars, not entire metal walls.

Thinking back, *I guess that could have been some kind of Taser. Or maybe I hit my head and dreamed every bit of it.*

I stand and make my way around the room, touching the walls and testing the floor. Everything is solid. There is no slowly-dying ping like when you knock on normal steel. This is like rapping your knuckles on concrete. No reverberation. And the walls are warm, which seems unusual. Though the air is warm as well, I expected the metal walls to be cool to the touch.

I move to the door, and still can find no way to open it from the inside. *Locked in,* I suppose. I walk back to the wall opposite the door and sit down. And worry. *What about my wife? My kids? My house? What will they think when I'm not home and the house is destroyed?* And I think about silly things too, like how I'm going to get water-damaged bamboo floors fixed when I can't buy bamboo anymore. I don't have my phone, so there's no way to call Brynn, no way to let her know what's going on. Even if I did have it, I'm in a metal box. I probably wouldn't have service anyway.

Just as I bury my face in my hands to cry, I hear what sounds like the push of an intercom button. And then the voice, seemingly coming from everywhere like the light, telling me to stay seated. "The door will open shortly," it says.

I keep my eyes peeled, focused on the door, ready to defend myself if necessary. I have no weapons, but if it's a fight for my life I'll make do with my hands. *Sure would be nice to know what the hell is going on,* I think. I hear the hiss of air, and the door slowly slides back an inch, then to the left, into the wall itself. There is no grinding of gears or clink of metal. The door seems to be the most well-maintained piece of equipment ever. The lighting outside the room is dull, again coming from everywhere and nowhere the same. It looks like a short hallway, empty, with the same metal covering every surface. There is another closed door at the end. The intercom cues up again, and tells me to step through the door.

I do as I'm told. Not out of choice, but from the lack thereof. As soon as I'm safely past the door, I hear it slide closed, the hiss of air sealing it shut again. Within seconds, I hear another hiss, but different this time, emanating from the grates beneath my feet. It sounds like air filling the room. I can smell it, though, and this is not normal oxygen. It has a chemical scent, and it is getting stronger with every breath. With no other options that I can think of, I immediately hold my breath as long as I can. The sound continues, assuring me that the chemical is still pumping in. Almost two minutes later, I give in, the instinctual urge to breathe overruling my will to hold it in. Letting out the huge breath burning in my chest, I instantly taste the chemical-rich air again.

Panicking now, I run to the next door, making it in four long strides. I beat my fists against it, screaming, "Let me out! What the hell is this?! Open the door!" A voice comes from everywhere again, telling me to stop struggling, and it will be over soon. This time, the breakdown comes. I squat against the wall and the tears flow freely, feeling odd mixed with the chemicals, running down my face. Thinking aloud, I tell my wife and kids that I love them and I'm sorry.

And then I hear the hiss of air slowly die off. Still concerned that I'm being poisoned, I check my skin for any sign of chemical burns. I can still breathe normally, and can't find anything wrong. As soon as the hiss ends, a great sucking noise begins. It sounds like air being pulled through a vacuum, but louder and with much more force. And then it quits as well. Standing again, I look to the third door as I hear the now familiar sound of it opening.

There's a man. He looks normal, except for his skin. There's something different about him, but in the dim light, I can't tell exactly what it is. His hair is average length and brown, covering a bit of his ears. Wearing what looks like tan linen pants and a matching shirt, he's standing completely still, his arms crossed over his chest. We both stand there a moment, silently appraising one another, both testing the threat level. He doesn't appear threatening though I can't place why I feel this way. His face is completely devoid of emotion, and his eyes reveal nothing. I know that my face and eyes must show everything, as I'm filled with fear and worry.

Finally, he speaks. "Follow me."

His voice sounds normal, but devoid of any accent. Like he learned English as a child, but from a computer. Silently, I do as I'm told. What reason do I have to do otherwise? I'm sure there are other men lurking just around a corner somewhere. And my intrigue is blocking out the rational parts of my brain. *Where is this place? What is this place? Why am I here? What the hell did I just endure in the last room?* I know that by following him, I have a chance of getting some answers.

As we walk, I begin to notice other oddities about my surroundings. The top of the walls curve into the ceiling, in the same gentle slope of the doors. There seem to be no real seams between any of it, other than at the floor. Every ten feet or so, I can see rivets, where one panel meets the next. It's almost as if I'm walking in a tube, and the space under the floor is used to carry the conduit and pipes I could see in the room I woke up in. And there are still no windows, *weird*, considering the tube-like feel of the hall I'm in. The level of background noise has stayed the same, making me think that the machines are above or below me somewhere.

We make a left turn at an intersection of hallways. I still haven't seen any other doors. I notice that I haven't seen any signs on the walls, or exit signs on the ceiling, either. *This must not be somewhere open to the public,* I realize. *Am I underground?*

We take a right at the next intersection, and I find myself in a hallway filled with doors. They each sit opposite each other, on the right and left, spaced about 8 feet apart all the way down the hallway. I can count at least ten on each side, but the dim light keeps me from seeing any further. After the fourth or fifth set, the man stops.

Turning to his left, the door opens automatically. On the other side is a room. It's small, but just as I imagined from the spacing of the doors in the hallway. Inside, there is only space for what appears to be a bed, with enough room to move around in front of it. At the foot sits a short metal chest with two drawers. *I don't even have anything to store in there.* On the metal frame sits what must be a mattress, but it looks thin. Resting at the far end of the mattress is a blanket, and a pillow at the end closest to me. The man gestures for me to step inside. As I do, he says "Rest. We will meet again soon."

"Wait," I say. "Tell me what's going on. Tell me anything."

"All will be explained shortly," the man tells me. "For now, this is where you will stay." With that, he steps into the hallway again, and the door shuts behind him.

"Why are they being so damn cryptic?!" I yell to myself. After I hear the hiss, I turn back to the room. More dim light comes from nowhere. Again, it is all metal with no window. It appears cleaner than the first room I was in, with no residual grime from years of constant use. There is an opening to my left. It looks like a doorway, but there is no door.

Stepping inside, the dim light comes on automatically. A metal toilet and sink face me, seeming oddly out of place in this environment. They appear clean at least, but still that bland grey color that matches everything else. On the left is what must be a shower. A nozzle drops a couple inches from the ceiling, and there is a metal button flush with the wall. A drain in the floor assures me that I'm correct. *At least I can clean myself,* I think.

I walk back into the bedroom, still clueless as to what is going on. In fact, I have even more questions than before. I can't figure out why I've been given a bedroom, or if my treatment should be seen as a good sign or bad. I sit on the mattress, hoping that my host will return soon. I need explanations, and I can feel my anxiety gathering more every minute.

As I sit, I hear the voice in the intercom again. "Rest," it says. "I will not return until you have done as I ask. All will be explained soon."

Frustrated, I look around. There is nothing here except a bed. No desk, no chairs, no TV or radio. Just metal walls and floor. It's becoming tiresome, everything being the same color. And confusing. *Why is* everything *metal?* I unfold the blanket at my feet, resigned to the fact that I won't leave this room without at least trying to sleep. I pull it up over me as I lay down, and notice that it feels like it's made of the same material as the clothes the man wore. Holding it between my fingers, it seems like it is the same linen, and I assume layers of it have been sewn together to create a fairly thick blanket. It's much softer than I thought it would be. The mattress is more comfortable than it looks, as is the pillow.

With the stress and anxiety of the day finally winning the battle raging in my head, I close my eyes.

I can tell that the already dim lights have turned off completely. Another question. *How do they work?* I lay there, thinking about the events that have transpired so far. I worry about Brynn and the kids. They must be terrified, knowing how they found the house. And now that they've realized I'm missing, I'm sure Brynn is frantic. Hell, *I* still can't wrap my brain around what has happened. *What was that ball of electricity? How did I get here from home? What is going on at home right now? And what is wrong with that guy's skin?* As my mind wandered, I slowly drifted off. Just as the man instructed, I finally slept.

· 3 ·

Questions
Unknown Location

IAWAKEN to the sound of a door opening and dim lights cutting on. Hours fly through my brain in seconds, and I quickly realize where I am, yet still have no idea *why*. I don't know how much time has passed, only that I feel surprisingly refreshed. Rolling onto my back and sitting up, I look over at the door and realize my host is standing in the doorway, wearing his typical tan clothes. I hold his gaze for a second before I mumble "Give me a minute," and amble into the bathroom. After I finish, I walk back into the room. The man is still standing in the doorway, patiently waiting for me. When I catch his gaze again, he tells me to follow him.

As before, I do as I'm told. We walk back the same way we came, and for a split second, I fear returning to the chemical room. We continue straight at the intersection, though, and keep moving down the long hallway. I breathe a small sigh of relief. It all looks the same as the other hallways, with its grimy grey walls and ceilings, ambient light, and a grated floor. From what I can tell so far, the place is enormous, with hallways shooting off in all four directions, continuing for what seems like impossible distances. *Some type of warehouse, maybe?*

Rounding another corner, I find three open doorways. I'm led into the center room, which appears to be about the size of the room I slept in. Inside, there is just a metal table with four metal chairs. It reminds me of an interrogation room, and my heart speeds up again. *What the hell is this?!*

"Sit," he tells me. "And you should calm down. Your heart rate has risen, and it serves you no purpose. There is no threat here."

Surprised, I ask, "How would you know my heart rate has risen?"

"I will return soon," he replies before the door closes behind him.

Frustrated again, I sit. Peering around the room, I notice it is the same as the others. I focus, studying every part of the chamber to pass the time. I notice something, and it feels like a breakthrough, no matter how insignificant. The rooms have solid floors while all of the hallways' floors are grated. The lighting in here is also brighter than the room I slept in, though still about the same as the hallways. I remind myself to keep looking for details.

Within five minutes, I hear the hiss of the opening door. The man enters, carrying a tray. On top sits a metal cup, bowl, and spoon. He sits down across from me and slides the tray to my side of the table. "Eat," he says.

"What is it?" I question.

"Food. It is safe. Just eat," he tells me. "Please. I understand that this is hard. Surely scary and confusing as well. But I can assure you that there is no risk to you here. We have nothing but your best interests in mind. Once you have eaten, I will personally make sure that you are brought up to speed with what is going on."

Having no real option but to trust my host, I grab the spoon. The contents of the bowl look almost like oatmeal, or grits. An off-white color, it's chunky, yet not solid. I lean down and sniff, and realize that it has no smell at all. I slide the spoon in, filling it with the thick paste. I lift it to my mouth and pause a second before taking my first nervous bite. The taste is surprising. It's faintly sweet, but with a hint of salt. Otherwise, there is nothing distinguishable about it. I stir it a bit and take another bite, and it still tastes the same. There's no real reason to chew though I do it out of habit anyways. Looking up, I catch the man's eye before he turns away. *Watching me eat?* I finish eating in just a few minutes, hungrier than I thought I was.

Squinting into the metal cup, it looks like water filling the inside. I take a tentative sip and confirm my thoughts. Downing the rest of the water, I set it down and push the tray to the center of the table. As the man stands and tells me to follow him, only one thought occurs to me. *Why would they have a single room with just a small table and chairs for visitors to eat in?*

He leads me out of the room, only to make an immediate right into the adjacent open doorway. When the lights come on upon us entering, I finally see something different. The room is perfectly round, and I'm standing on a landing. There is a spiral staircase in the center. It is wide, and looks like two people could pass comfortably without having to move over. We start up without pause. I notice immediately that there is no sound. Just like the walls, you could stomp on these thin metal stairs with no reverberations. Looking up, I can see another landing above our heads. The floors appear to be the same size as those in an ordinary building. We exit the stairs on the first landing we come to. I look up again, and realize the stairs continue up to at least one more level.

Stepping into the hallway, I'm surprised to see other men milling about. There are open and closed doors, with people passing through all of them. They all wear varying colors of the same clothes. At the end of the hall, I can see an opening, and the room beyond looks brightly lit compared to everything I've seen so far.

We head in that direction, and I notice that everyone that has looked at me has let their eyes linger for a little longer than normal before they continue what they're doing. They don't seem aggressive, but it's still uncomfortable. They all have the same odd skin as well, but otherwise, look like the average person. "The hell are you looking at?" I mumble to averted eyes as we pass, irritated that everyone seems to be staring. *Did I miss my mouth at breakfast?*

As we pass the open rooms, I glance inside each one. One appears to be storage, with metal shelves evenly spaced inside. Gleaming boxes fill the shelves, and a man inside pulls one off while we pass. In a room on the right, I see what looks like a kitchen. Something resembling a grill sits against the back wall, with a pile of the paste I just ate steaming in the middle. There are shelves on the left and right walls, with stacks of trays, cups, and utensils on each. Another room contains more metal shelves, each filled with large white cylindrical containers. Two more rooms have signs on the doors, the first I've seen. An unusual looking 'male' and 'female' picture are centered in each door. They don't look like the restroom signs I'm used to seeing, but nothing about this place is normal so far. Nearing the room at the end of the hallway, my anticipation begins to grow. The brighter lighting alone makes me think this room must be more significant than the others.

Finally, outside the bright room, my host stops. Turning to me, he says, "Once we enter this room, you must remain calm and keep your mind open. This is the only way you can understand." I nod my head in agreement, and he turns back to the door. We walk in, and the door closes behind us.

The first thing I notice is the cleanliness. This

room seems spotless. The walls and ceiling shine as if brand new. This, I realize, is why the room seems brighter. They are reflecting the light back into the room, lighting up like the daylight outside. I still can't find a source of the light, though. Thinking about this, it reminds me of the ball of electricity I encountered at home. This room is also much larger than any others I have seen so far. It's easily half of a football field in length and width, and must be at least two stories tall.

Two rows of cubicles sit along the left side. I see keyboards, which make me think these must be computer terminals, but there aren't any processors or monitors. *Strange,* I think. *Where are the rest of the components?* On the other side of the room are what look like servers. Rows of tall, black, rectangular pillars shoot up from the floor. I can hear the whirring of hard drives and smell the scent of hot electrical components. Lights blink away on each, the always present sign of information being transferred. The center of the room has rows of tables, some of which have items on top though I can't tell what they are. I see a few of the cylindrical containers from earlier. A few others have what looks like thick electrical wire, but the coating doesn't look like rubber. *Some type of non-conductive metal, maybe?* The far wall, directly across from me, has nothing near it. The floor, white metal again, is empty of anything, except for two other people standing in the center.

My host leads me that way. Walking by the tables, I see that it is, in fact, some type of metal coating the wires I noticed. The containers are metal as well, but painted. *Or is that a weird naturally white metal?* They seem to be doing something, as I can feel the heat emanating from them as we pass. Making our way to the end of the tables and entering the empty space, I am struck again by how large this room really is. Looking over my shoulder, the door now seems so far away. No one has entered after us either.

I'm still not used to not hearing an echo. A room this size should have sound bouncing off of every wall, but it seems to be absorbed instead. As we near the other two men, they turn from us and start walking. They head in the same direction we do, toward the one empty wall. Breaking the silence in the last few steps before we stop, I ask, "What is this place?"

"Are you prepared for the answer?" My host questions. "Very few have been as prepared as they thought. We expect your response to be one of astonishment, and we are sure that you will have more questions than you already do. Your heart rate and blood pressure will rise to a much higher level, as will your temperature. You will have an unusually high level of synapses firing in your brain, which may induce headaches. You may also begin the fight or flight process though we aren't expecting this reaction from you. We know you have no health risks, but if you would like, we can supply you with a chair."

I answer only, "Yes," pushing away the questions he has already added to my ever growing list. We complete our trek across the bright room. The two men in front stop, and my host steps between them. They turn to face me, all wearing the same blank expression. Each of the additional men is wearing blue linen clothes, while my host wears tan. Their shoes all match, with what seems like just thick cloth surrounding each foot.

The new men look older than my host, but each has the same odd skin everyone else has. With the better lighting, I can see now that it appears almost opaque, with a greyness that is unlike any other skin I've ever seen. It looks healthy, as if this were just another natural skin color. I notice now that their eyes are all the same color, but sit just a little farther apart than normal. Their noses are longer and thin, but with tiny nostrils. Their lips are thin as well, but their mouths otherwise appear normal. Their ears sit higher on their heads than mine. All of this leaves me with yet more unanswered questions.

"Okay then. My name is Kalis. I am the chief scientific officer. The man to my left is Birkim, our psychological engineer. And to my right is Alter, the Captain." My heart rate immediately quickens at the mention of a Captain. "You are currently standing in our operational viewing room, room 17A, on Deck 11." With that, he turns from me. "Alter, will you please disengage the display block so that our guest may see where he is?"

While my brain reels at this new bit of information, Alter walks to the wall. My ideas of what is happening seems ridiculous to me. None of what I've learned is coming together to form a valid thought. *Captain? Operational Viewing Room? Deck 11?* The odd names, the odd bodies. I can't grasp what it all means. The ideas in my head seem so far from rational. Alter, using his foot, presses a button that is flush with the floor. The entire wall in front of me begins to slide up and away, somehow folding into the ceiling above me. What is on the other side freezes those thoughts instantly. My heart rate and blood pressure rise. I can feel the heat of adrenaline coursing through my body. Extra synapses fire, with the immediate thrum of a headache. My feet, however, stay rooted in place.

"Welcome to our ship, the Zavilisk, currently maintaining position in Galaxy SVM-145 in the Shapley Supercluster."

·4·

Answers

The Zavilisk, SVM-145

W*HAT. The. Hell.* I think, staring out the window. "We're in fucking space?!"

"Yes," replies Kalis, in his typical monotone voice. "Surprised?"

"You could say that." I inch closer to the window, wanting to see down, but scared to lean too far. The realizations hit me at once. Why everything is made of metal. The slop I ate. The long halls, with airtight doors. The absence of windows. The ever-present distant humming that must be engines and compressors, all kinds of machinery needed to operate something this large. Even the chemical room makes sense now. It must have been some type of cleansing process, used to remove whatever microbes I brought here from

Earth. I still have many questions, but at least I am finally getting somewhere.

"We know you have more questions, but we will get to those soon. Right now, we just want you to relax. Your heart rate still needs to come down some." says Birkim. "Enjoy the view. Not many from Earth have seen it."

Not many from Earth? As in I'm not the first? I look out into the vast darkness before me with a sense of vertigo like none other. I can see what must be distant galaxies, nothing more than pinpricks of light, hovering far away. I think back to my research. It's amazing to see other galaxies here the same way we see stars from Earth. *The Shapley Supercluster. It's pretty far from the Virgo, universally speaking, with the Centaurus Supercluster splitting the two. How in the hell did I get here,* hundreds *of light years from home?* "You're aliens," I say, disbelief still evident in my voice.

"Well, right now, on *our* ship, I would say that you are the alien, Ira," the Captain says, eyebrows raised.

"Okay, okay. Jesus. You're right," I reply, pausing. "I think I'm ready for some explanations now," I say, turning to look at Kalis. The other two eye me closely, as if making sure I won't run. "Please. I won't be *able* to calm down until I understand more."

"Okay. Please, follow me." Kalis replies. We turn to the left and walk. The servers are getting closer now, and their size becomes more apparent. While I'm sure that this is what they are, their massive size throws me off. *Are they really bad at processing information, or can they process more than half of the servers on Earth combined?* I settle on the latter. Nothing inefficient would be on a ship like this. I now notice a door on the wall behind them, making me wonder how many more doors I've missed in the operational viewing room. We head towards it, and it opens before we get there.

Inside, it looks something like a lounge. There are low sitting chairs, all situated around tables, with more open windows to my left. The walls are shiny, making this space bright like the great room we just left. It's starting to look as if common areas are kept brightly lit, while others are not. On the wall, I can see images, but they look artificial. Just like the holograms I envisioned. The floors are white like the great room as well, and again carry no sound.

"Have a seat," the Captain tells me, having already sat in the chair beside the one he gestured me to. I sit, and Kalis sits across from me. Birkim, the "psychological engineer,' *whatever the hell that is*, sits beside him in the last remaining seat.

"Okay, please, tell me what's going on."

"Well, Ira, there are only certain things we can tell you right now. Others will have to wait," says Kalis.

"Why?" I ask. "What's the difference? I can't imagine I'd have any different reaction later versus now."

"You may very well be correct," Birkim says, watching me intently. "But we need to figure that out for ourselves, rather than just laying everything on the table and leaving it to chance."

"You already know where you are," the Captain adds. You know that you are aboard our ship, the Zavilisk -"

"Yeah, the ship." I interrupt. "How big is this thing, anyway?"

"We don't measure in your feet or meters, so it is not very practical for us to try to explain how large it is, is it? In time, you'll get a feel for how big it is." replies the Captain.

Dammit, he's right, I realize, thinking about what I want to ask next. I have so many questions; I can't pick which is the most important.

"Why don't you let us just talk. We'll tell you what we can, and you can ask us questions after." Says Kalis. "I think that would be the easiest for all of us."

"Okay. Talk."

"Okay. To start, our species is Ralsik. We look much like you humans do, and that is not without reason. Think about this for a second. Your path of evolution is fairly normal throughout the universe. Most carbon-based life forms have traveled the same path, because of the environment they thrive in. Planets that are in their star's 'sweet spot,' as you have called it, have much the same features universe wide. Oxygen, nitrogen, minerals, water, vegetation. Those are all basic elements required for carbon-based life to exist. So, it is only natural for these planet's inhabitants to go through the same evolutionary phases. From sea creature to land mammal, to walking on two legs and gaining enough knowledge to build. It happens everywhere." He pauses, letting this sink in. "We all may look a little different, naturally. Our DNA is not the same. Planetary features like water do not dictate how high our ears sit. But rest assured, you will recognize almost all intelligent life in the universe as looking surprisingly... related.

"Some species, of course, don't make it. This can be caused by warring, asteroid strikes, or changes in their planet's structure or orbit, to name a few. There are many reasons, and not all can be planned for in advance. And some species just may not have enough knowledge to combat the natural events that can happen, like asteroid impacts. Unfortunately, we have lost many advanced species over the course of time.

"And, on that note, I'll add one last bit about intelligent life. Your percentages in your article were off."

"Wait. What do you mean, off?" I ask. "How could you possibly know how many planets in the universe host life?"

"*How* is not important right now, Ira. Basics, remember?" Birkim adds.

"Okay, but seriously. Off? In what way?"

"Your percentage of planets in the habitable zone that actually do have life, Ira. It's low. Very low."

"What?! Low? Like, how low?"

"Your number should be much closer to one. Approximately one-half of a percent, to be exact," states Kalis, his eyes finally showing some life.

My mind spins in circles. *One-half of a percent? That's insane! That would mean the universe is teeming with life.* "What about the number of habitable planets in general?" I ask. "How many of those are there?"

"Do not worry about that quite yet, Ira," Kalis says. "Is the knowledge that there are billions of inhabited planets in the universe not enough?"

"No, no, it's plenty," I reply. "It's just so unexpected. I honestly thought that my percentages were still high."

"If it helps, some of those planets were settled by species' that already existed elsewhere," Birkim says. "Not all of them had life to begin with. The universe is a sensitive place. Small changes may result in no life at all, though all of the basic necessities are there."

Settled, I think. *There are so many advanced civilizations out there, some are settling on other planets, just because they can.*

"We call a planet here in SVM-145 home," Alter adds. "We typically spend most of our adult lives here on this ship, though. Once you become an officer here, it is a mission that requires the dedication of a lifetime."

"Why?" I ask. "Why do you need to spend your whole life here? Why can't someone else on your planet train for your job and take over?"

"Because not many are suited for what we do, Ira."

"And what exactly is it that you do?"

"Well, deal with brink civilizations like yours, of course," Birkim replies.

Huh? "Brink civilizations?"

"We will get into that later. I promise, soon enough, you will have more understanding than anyone alive on Earth. Give it time." Kalis says.

More comfortable giving them the time they ask, for now, I agree to change subjects. "How did we get here from Earth?"

"I can give you an idea, but no details. Will that be enough? This is one of the subjects that I am bound by universal law not to elaborate on," Alter says.

"Yes, of course. That's fine. I can wait." *Universal law?*

"Well, I'm sure you remember the events leading up to you waking up on the ship?" Kalis asks.

"How could I forget?" I retort. "And, by the way, the bare rooms and gas chamber aren't exactly a good way to treat a guest."

"Yes, we apologize for that," Replies Alter, sincerely. "But you have to understand, it is for the safety of the members of our ship. Some have been known to wake up violently. And some are much stronger than you or I. The first room was designed to isolate you while you regained your senses. Kalis was in control and monitoring you the entire time. The 'gas chamber'," he continues, "contained an air-dispersed chemical designed to remove any biological organisms that cannot safely exist on this ship. Once the cycle was complete, that mixture was removed from the room and replaced with clean air. There was never any risk to your safety, unless it was your own actions that caused it."

"The way in which you found yourself on the Zavilisk, unfortunately, is the only way to get here. If we were in your solar system, or even in your galaxy, it would have been much less strenuous. We cannot be seen inside of your solar system, though. So your journey was much more difficult than that of others before you," Kalis begins. "Our ship was in a neighboring galaxy, Andromeda, when you were brought here. We traveled to our home galaxy immediately afterward.

"To get onto our ship, we used an extraction system designed millions of years ago. Essentially, electricity is combined with dark matter to create a tunnel in which you traveled. I honestly don't know everything about it. I wasn't the designer, obviously, and the system is proprietary. It is installed at a ship owner's request, by the only species that makes it. Basically, space is warped, creating a doorway. On one side is you, and on the other is our isolation room. The doorway is opened, you are pulled through, and then it is closed again. We apologize for the mess we created in your home."

"Currently, I think it's worth it. I just hope I don't learn anything that changes my mind," I reply. "How did we get here from Andromeda? That's a bit of a drive."

"That is one thing I can't tell you for certain, Ira.

We stopped existing in the Andromeda Galaxy while at the same moment in time, we began our existence again here in SVM-145. Honestly, it is basically the same process as we use to bring people aboard the ship. Just at a much larger scale. I'm sorry, I can't tell you any more at this time," replied Alter. He actually seemed saddened by having to tell me so little.

"Well, if that's the case, can I get a tour?"

"Of course! Our ship is fairly basic," Alter states nonchalantly, as we set off through the operational viewing room again. "Most of the levels house rooms for people to sleep. The others have laboratories, offices, things like that. A few decks for mechanical. Deck 1, on the bottom, is our loading bay. Vehicles and smaller aircraft are stored there in the hangar, along with the emergency escape modules. The deck you found yourself on, 11, is dedicated to you, and others like you. A lot goes into bringing someone like you on board, Ira. We don't take it lightly. Deck 12 is where you are now," Captain Alter elaborated. "Mostly just the operational viewing room, and its support. Food, restrooms, and offices for the personnel that work in here. The viewing room itself is for, well, viewing. It offers the best view of the space ahead of us. We prefer that basic studies happen here, focusing mainly on space. We allow just about anything to be done here, though, when no studies are taking place. We understand how mesmerizing and motivating the view can be. Deck 13, the top deck, is the cockpit and its support. Navigation, boost, proximity, things like that. Would you like to see?"

"Of course," I say, as we enter the giant spiral stairwell. As we begin our ascension, I notice something here that I didn't before. The stair treads seem to have a rough texture, for grip I assume. But there is no distinct difference in appearance from the other metal that surrounds us.

Reaching the landing, we step out into a room even more expansive than the last. Spanning what must be the length and width of the ship, it is filled with machinery. Opaque screens are everywhere. Some on walls, and others seemingly hovering in the middle of the room, nothing around but people, pecking and clicking at keyboards in their laps while they sit. The floor of the room is the same white metal, and the walls are the same brightness as those in the viewing room one level down. To my right are the forward facing viewing windows, the only indication of which is their size. They are the same size as the windows below, while all the others in the room are smaller. We head to the left, where I assume we will find the rear of the ship.

"Most of these people are system engineers," Alter tells me as we pass by floating screens and men and women lost in their tasks. "They are ensuring that everything is running smoothly. On the other side," he gestures to the right, "are the telemetry and guidance specialists. They make sure we are headed in the right direction, and all the systems required for that are communicating correctly." As we near the rear of the ship, more large windows come into view. "Here is our gravity department. These men and women ensure our artificial gravity is operational, and change it to suit the atmospheres we enter and exit." Passing them, we make it to the end of the pathway we've been walking. "Back here, my Lieutenant controls our motion when we move in reverse. We don't do it often, as you can imagine, in a ship this size. It requires a high amount of skill, though, as there is not as much thrust or boost dedicated to moving backward."

We turn around and head back the way we came. As we walk, I'm given time to take in my surroundings. The men and women on this level are completely dedicated to their tasks. Immersed in what they are doing, they don't even notice as we pass. *No one is this dedicated at home,* I notice, studying the faces of the people we pass. Eyes aren't even lifted in our direction. *I can only imagine how efficient they must be.* One man, crossing the path from one side of the room to the other, makes eye contact. I'm almost startled by it, seeing how intent everyone else was on their work. He actually waves as we pass, and I think I see a small smile. *So they* do *have emotions,* I laugh to myself. Passing the stairwell in the distance to our right, Alter begins describing his workplace once more.

"This is our navigation department," he tells me while we pass large screens displaying what must be asteroids, stars, and everything in between. "They are constantly making adjustments to our course, based on the space we are in. It is quite a chore, re-routing the ship around ever asteroid we pass. And the work that goes into setting and verifying coordinates thousands or millions of lightyears away is immeasurable." Ahead, I can see that we are approaching the front of the ship. In the center, only feet from the windows, is a pilot-like seat, raised above the floor on a platform of about 8 feet by 3 feet. The chair, I can see now, can slide from one end of the station to the other. In front of the platform is a console, filled to the max with buttons and screens and levers. Each must have an important function, but it is lost on me. I have no what any of these controls must be. To the left and right of the platform, stretching to both walls, are more consoles. These are manned by numerous people, steadily walking back and forth, checking a screen here and pushing a button there.

"This," Alter says with noticeable excitement as we reach the platform, "is the heart of the Zavilisk. I'm actually not needed here much. I come up occasionally to check our course and ensure that all systems are operating properly. My duties as Captain make me needed everywhere aboard the ship. The only time I have to be here is if there is a problem, or when we are docking or lifting off. There are a few other times, of course, some of which I can't go into detail with you. Rest assured, though, that the ship is always in good hands. The men and women on this level are some of the most highly trained available."

"This is amazing," I utter, slowly spinning, still trying to take it all in. "I never imagined it would take so many people to operate a ship that could move through deep space. I'm speechless."

"Need some more time?" Kalis asks, watching me take in the room.

"No, no, this is fine. I don't think more time would really help me take all this in anyways." I tell him, eliciting a grin from both Kalis and Alter.

"Let us get you back to your room for the evening then," suggests Birkim. "We can continue our discussions tomorrow."

Nodding in agreement, we begin the long walk back to my room. After seeing and learning so much today, I really am ready to get some rest. To pass the time, we make small talk. I tell them about my family and home, and ask random questions about things or places we pass.

Before I knew it, we are back outside the doorway to my room. As it opens, I turn to Kalis. "So we'll do this again tomorrow?" I ask, unsure of what to expect.

"Yes," he responds, holding his hand to my open door. "But rest tonight. You're going to need it for the rest of your journey. There won't be anything strenuous, but your mind needs to remain fresh. I will see you in the morning." With that, he turns from me and walks back the way we came, catching up with Birkim and Alter, who stopped at the end of the hallway.

After I enter to room, the door closes behind me. I lay down on the bed immediately, feeling exhausted. The day plays over and over again in my head, touching on the answers, and creating more questions. One question, though, looms larger than the rest. Surprised that I haven't asked them yet, I ask myself, *why am I here?*

· 5 ·
Revelation
The Zavilisk SVM-145

W AKING up the next morning, I feel much better. I slip from the bed and head into the bathroom, deciding to figure out the shower. I drop my clothes and step under the nozzle. After pushing the button in the wall, hot water rains down on me. I stand there and soak it in, probably for much longer than I should. Reanalyzing the information I was given yesterday, I renew my vow to dig deeper today. I push the recessed button again, and the water stops flowing. *I'm figuring this place out, dammit,* I think as I step out from under the nozzle and into the floor.

Studying my appearance in the mirror, I realize it's been almost 3 days since I've shaved. I'm not used to it. At home, I keep my face clean. *Do they shave?* I wonder. I haven't paid enough attention to their faces to know. Maybe they'll have a razor for me. I'm looking a little rough.

I grab my clothes and walk back into the bedroom, letting the air dry my body before I get dressed again. Turning to the bed, I notice a neat stack of blue linen clothes waiting for me. *How'd they get in here without me noticing?* Shrugging, I put my old clothes down and reach for the fresh pile. It turns out they are the same material as the blanket, just as I suspected. I put them on, finding them much more comfortable than they initially looked.

Turning around to face the room, I prepare to sit on the bed and wait. Instead, as if on cue, the door to my room begins to open. *I'll have to ask them how they do that,* I remind myself. Kalis enters, and I can see Birkim waiting in the hallway.

"Good morning, Ira," says Kalis, with more emotion than I am used to. "Ready to start our day?"

"Yes, of course," I tell him. It's the truth. I'm hungry for new information like I'm hungry for food.

"Let us get started, then," Kalis replies as we start to walk.

As we travel, we make more small talk. "How did you sleep?" Birkim asks.

I immediately wonder if he's using his profession right now. *Is he analyzing me?* "I slept well, thanks. Surprisingly well, actually. I was concerned when I saw the bedroom and mattress the first night. And the blanket looks much thinner than it really is. It's all much more comfortable than I thought it would be.

And I think all this information just builds and builds all day, so when I finally get into the bed at night, I crash," I tell him honestly.

"This is normal," he states, as we begin to cross the operational viewing room. "Most visitors in your position are the same. We've had some sleep for days after learning all you have."

"I have no doubt," I reply, realizing that I, too, could sleep for days if I really wanted to. I take in the view ahead of me as we walk. The darkness, as scary as it is, is beautiful. I study the distant stars as we begin to turn, heading to the lounge behind the servers again. *That's what makes it beautiful,* I realize. *The light within the darkness.*

We enter the lounge and take our seats, and I find a bowl of food waiting for me. I eat quickly, wanting to jump right into today's topics. Downing my water, I look up to see both men watching me. "What?" I ask.

"You eat very quickly," Birkim states.

"Yeah well, that's what we do where I'm from. When we are excited about something, we have a habit of speeding through everything else."

"I understand. It seems like a reasonable enough behavior." Birkim replies.

"I have a question," I state. "What is your purpose here, Birkim? I keep thinking about it, and I can't find any reason to need a psychological 'engineer' on board a ship like this."

"I'm here for you, Ira," he begins. "*You* are my job here. We will talk more, later. I have many questions for you."

"Can I ask another question?"

"Of course, anything. I just can't guarantee you an answer," Kalis tells me.

"How do you always seem to know what I'm thinking? And you are always aware of when I'm ready to leave my room. How is that?"

"Well," Birkim begins, "We don't actually know what you're thinking. One trait the Ralsiks do have, though, is the ability to analyze different features and inputs, and combine them into logic very quickly. We use this to our advantage when interacting with our visitors.

"When you are reacting to an input or thinking," he continues, "you give off subtle cues. Your muscles around your mouth may contract or loosen. Your eyebrows raise or lower, as do your ears. Your eyes may shift, even slightly. Your body temperature can rise or fall, causing your pores to tighten and create 'goosebumps,' or you may sweat a little.

"We take all of this information, and then combine it with intuition. How might someone feel when we tell them this fact? What might they think? If I were in your position, what would my immediate reaction be?

"Added together with the visual indicators, this gives us what we need. It usually works quite well for us."

I think about this for a second. It makes sense. An ability I'm envious of, for sure. They seem to be the masters of critical thinking.

Diving straight into my next question, I ask, "Where does the light come from?"

"Aah, we knew this would be coming sooner or later," Kalis replies. "For us, it is not complicated. Just another piece of normal technology. Light can be manipulated in many more ways than you understand, Ira. The light in this room, like all the others, does not come from anywhere. It just exists.

"As I'm sure you've noticed, we are able to keep it at low levels in most areas. It is better for vision. In the areas where brightness is important, though, the metal is polished, causing it to reflect more of the light than in other rooms."

"It just exists? Everyone on earth thinks it is impossible to manipulate energy in ways that seem normal for you. How many years are you ahead of us, anyway? As a species."

"Many more than you'd expect," Birkim tells me.

"But that is not important," Kalis adds. "I cannot tell you why at this moment, but I can assure you that soon you will understand how insignificant the number of years ahead of you, we are."

"Okay," I reply, not sure what else to say. "Now, about that metal. What is it? It's different than anything I've ever seen before."

"That's because it's not something that could ever be produced on Earth," Kalis says, watching me as my eyes scan the floor around us. "It is a pretty special material, really. It is extremely strong. Stronger than anything you can make with materials from Earth. It is also malleable, as you may have noticed with the wiring on the tables in the viewing room. Its properties are dictated by the temperatures used to make it. Cooler temperatures make it flexible while higher temperatures make it rigid. It also acts as a barrier to sound. I'm sure you've heard the silence when you walk, or noticed the fact that nothing echoes. The color variations come from the planets it is mined from.

"There are a few planets far away from here where we can get it. They are not habitable, so they are used solely for mining purposes. It works out well. No one group owns them in any way. We are just expected to take what we need.

"This is how it is with most things in the universe," he adds. "The planets we live on are used only for living. We keep them clean and in turn, they give us what we need. Life. Sustenance. Safety.

"The planets that no one could live on are treated differently. When one is discovered, it is tested. This process takes years, but it is necessary. We ensure that there is no life on the planet, first. After that, we take samples. We test for minerals that we can use, and minerals that are toxic. Once these tests are complete and have positive results, we test the conditions of the space around it. We ensure that no other planets or moons would be affected by drilling and mining. Only after all of this is complete, do we begin mining a planet. If even a single of our variables is not met, we leave it be."

"I'm still processing, sorry," I say as I notice them

staring at me. "I'm a little awestruck at the idea of mining entire planets. When you say 'we,' you just mean your species, correct?"

"No," says Birkim. "The people of the universe. There are agreed upon standards."

"Agreed upon standards? The other species communicate with each other?"

"Yes," explains Kalis. "Not in your English, of course, but in other languages. We have consolidated down to just a few languages we use throughout the universe when dealing with other species. They each are free to have their own language. But like English is the business language of Earth, we only have a few 'business' languages in the universe as well. We learned English just to speak with you."

"Woah," I think out loud. "Just for me? I thought you said that there have been others as well?"

"Yes, there have been. But this was long before we took over the ship. We can cover that later," replies Birkim, his eyes meeting my gaze. "Soon you will be ready to understand more of what we are doing here."

"Okay. How do you have water here?" I ask.

"We make it here. Basic chemistry shows that you get water by mixing hydrogen and oxygen," Kalis tells me, as if I should have known already.

I nod my head, this bit of information seeming to be the most normal thing I've heard since I got here. "What about the food we eat? What is that?"

"The food is simple as well. There are things our bodies need for sustenance each day. The food contains all of them. The vitamins, minerals, correct amounts of protein. All of it is there. Even sugar and salt, which I'm sure you can taste. The absence of color is because there is nothing artificial in it. Everything serves a purpose. This way, it is easy for us to store large amounts of ingredients on board at a time. The ingredients that are needed are typically harvested on our home planet," he adds. "If there is a species that doesn't produce one of the ingredients, their diets typically do not require it. It is rare, but it does happen. Most carbon-based life in the universe requires the same basic compounds."

"That makes sense," I say. "I was honestly surprised it had any taste at all." My mind wandering again, I think of my next question.

"You mentioned artificial gravity yesterday. How do you do that? Scientists on Earth have said that it is impossible."

"This, unfortunately," Kalis begins, "Is another one of those pieces of information that we cannot tell you. I hope you understand by now that we have reasons for this. And I hope you trust that our reasons are sound. We will be able to explain further soon."

"Okay. Tell me about the way this universal society. How does it work? How did it come to be?"

"Well," Birkim starts, eyeing Kalis before continuing, "It functions like any normal community you'd expect. In fact, that is what we call it. The community. It functions peacefully for the most part. Advanced civilizations don't war with other people on their planets. Once a species reaches this level of enlightenment, wars become obsolete. Fighting with our own species does not advance the species in any way.

"Multiple planets realizing this around the same time is what initially lead to the larger universal civilization. Sure, in the beginning, there were small quarrels between people. There were those who refused to conform to the new concept of being united as a planet. With time, though, this subsided. Eventually, these worlds had many years of peace. When functioning as one people, instead of smaller factions, they were able to accomplish tasks and gain a greater understanding of the world around them much faster.

Years later," he continues, "one of these planets figured out the mysteries of deep space travel. Keep in mind, this was preceded by many advancements in other technologies. They set their sights on another planet in their galaxy that showed signs of life. It was in its star's habitable zone, and its carbon signature and atmosphere appeared to have been changed through artificial means. They traveled to this planet.

"I'm sure you can imagine their astonishment when the inhabitants looked surprisingly like themselves. Through the use of technology and plenty of basic hand signals, they figured out ways to communicate. They shared technologies and valuable lessons learned. They shared resources that neither had seen before. Food, vegetation, tools and techniques, everything was transferred as knowledge from one group of people to the next."

Birkim pauses, letting the information served thus far sink in before starting again. "Within just a few decades, the host planet was able to travel, the same as their guests. While each maintained a distinct style in which they produced and designed things, the basic technologies shared brought them together.

"They created a pact, both vowing to search for other advanced life forms, capable of doing exactly what they did. Now, over the course of millions of years, many other species have been able to gain the knowledge of the universe. It has surely been beneficial for all." He finishes this slowly and quietly, which makes the message impact me even harder.

Speechless. Again. It's happening more and more these days. I don't know what to say. I wasn't nearly as prepared for an explanation as I thought. The deeper meaning of it all is what really strikes home, considering what is happening to the United States right now. *How could we ever hope to achieve anything this grand, when we can't even keep the people in our own country happy?* I wonder, feeling disappointed.

"I need a minute," I state, sliding from my seat. I walk over to the large windows and look out over the vast empty space before me. *What has become of the world I live in,* I wonder. *How can we as a people allow this to happen? We are slowly killing our planet. Slowly killing its inhabitants, with pollution and disease. We are losing sight of the very thing that can save us. Reason. The bigger picture. Our people keep thinking about only themselves. The governments do the same thing. When we should be coming together, we continue to drift farther apart. How can we ever hope to become this advanced? This peaceful? At this rate, we will destroy our planet and ourselves before we ever have a chance of learning even the most basic universal facts.* A tear slips down my cheek as I take in the majestic view. I can feel it so surely now. I'm positive that I will be the last person from Earth to ever see something quite as amazing as this. I wipe my face, still wondering where we go from here.

With the view and my recent revelation, my final question comes to mind. I feel ridiculous asking it now. Embarrassed even. Embarrassed for my relation to the other inhabitants of Earth. Saddened by all of the damage we have caused. I feel a twinge of anger, too. It feels almost like they're mocking me by bringing me here, all the while knowing that the people of Earth could never see such greatness. But, I choose to ask my question anyway. I have nothing to lose at this point. And, surely, after all of this, I at least deserve some sort of explanation.

So, with my resolve set, I ask, "Why am I here?"

Birkim and Kalis slowly look at each other, a small smile forming on Kalis' thin lips. Softly, he replies, "We've been waiting for you to ask that. We want your help."

· 6 ·
Unique
The Zavilisk, SVM-145

I LOOK to each of them, my eyes slowly moving from Kalis to Birkim. If I thought I had figured anything out before, the idea is gone again. *Need my help?* I can't imagine that there would be anything at all I could do to help a species such as this, so far advanced that I'm currently sitting in a supercluster two away from my own.

"How in the world could I possibly help you?" I question them both, anxiously awaiting whatever impossible reason they have.

"Ira, now is the time that I must ask you again if you are prepared for the answer you will receive. I am confident in you as our choice, but I need to make sure that you feel ready to learn something that will be quite a shock," Birkim says.

"I'm as ready as I'll ever be," I state flatly.

"There exists a council of sorts, within the universal community," Kalis starts. "This council, upon receiving information and updates from research ships such as the Zavilisk, makes decisions regarding planets that appear to be ready for contact. If it is decided that a planet is not ready, we leave their proximity and come to our home planet for rest and refit. The planet will be studied again in a half century or so. We then set out for the next. If a planet is indeed deemed ready for us to make contact, it is myself and Birkim that do so.

"Upon arriving, we would seek out world leaders. This is when the sharing begins. We allow them to analyze our technologies, and walk them through the engineering and design processes, ensuring that they can comprehend what we are showing them. We teach them about the universe, about the separate species and the community, and help them understand what is necessary to become a part of the larger social structure. We advise them on what needs to happen before they can join us in space, like making real plans to rid their planet of pollution, ending famine and war, and completing the process of coming together as one species.

"From there," he continues, "we help them assemble a council of their own. Scientists, psychologists, the world leaders and others, are all brought together. We allow them to decide for themselves, after viewing all of the facts and information we have given them, if their species as a whole is ready to assume their place in the universal community.

"Some have, in fact, decided that they weren't ready. They are then given a single piece of technology. A means to communicate with our council directly. When they feel they are prepared, they notify the council, and another envoy is sent to their planet. Once we ensure the standards have been met, they are then assisted in joining us in space.

"The ones that do initially decide to join us are immediately aided, with our people and tools helping them achieve the advancements in science and engineering that would have taken hundreds, if not thousands, more years without our help."

"My job in the process," Birkim interjects, "Is to learn about and monitor their emotional state. I help them mentally, when they need it, just as Kalis helps them scientifically. I also lead in advising them on what to expect, and ensure that they can understand what is happening and will happen. People are fragile, emotionally and physically. Someone like myself is necessary to ensure that their journey goes as smoothly as possible. And, if at any time, I decide that a species is not mentally stable enough to join the universal community, then we leave. They would then be viewed again as candidates in 50 years, as we said before, and visited shortly after."

Kalis now, looking directly at me, says, "The reason we seek your help, Ira, is because until recently, we were only a few years away from making contact with Earth."

"What?!" I exclaim, surprised by this admission, so out of place with my previous thoughts. "How could you be considering Earth?! We destroy our planet daily. Someone is always at war with someone else. We can barely get to Mars!"

"Were, Ira. I said 'were.' We *were* going to make contact with Earth."

My heart pounding in my chest now, tears threatening to flow again, I ask, "Why not now? What changed?"

"Your country, Ira," Birkim responds. "The leaders of the free world, suddenly, have become a shining example of what a species was never meant to do. Your country went from world leaders to an entirely introverted society in less than a year. We cannot overlook that."

"But," Karim adds, "This is the reason we brought you here. After reviewing our information, the notes we've taken over the years, and our knowledge of your species, we decided that bringing a visitor aboard may allow us to make contact with your planet still. There is one thing that still shines brightly, the history of it much more powerful than its current absence.

"Your species, Ira, more than any other we have studied before, possesses the power to come together as one whenever need be, with speed not seen anywhere else. And not just to aid each other in war. With other things as well, like pollution control, stopping the unnatural warming of your atmosphere, responding to threats from space.

"The people, as well," he continues. "There are not many other planets in the universe where people value other people's safety and well-being more than their own. Sure, there are species that will aid their friends, but nothing like the people of Earth. Never before have we seen people jumping in front of moving vehicles to save another life, or giving their organs to help another live.

"This uniqueness needs to be brought to the universal stage. Other species can learn from this. Compassion this thorough and deep is rarely seen, and never from an entire species. And what makes it so powerful, is that you do not even know it is abnormal. To your species, this is regular, even expected, behavior. The universe needs this, Ira. And we want you to help us."

With this, Birkim says, "The council actually sent us back to retrieve a visitor. We explained to them our predicament, and they saw so much potential in your species that they waived, for the first time ever, the minimum wait of half a century and sent us back to see if we can assist in making changes."

"So here we are," Kalis finishes.

"I don't even know where to begin," I say, honestly lost. My mind is still reeling from the revelation that there is a process to all of this, that these advanced societies seek out growing species and aid them when the time comes. That the entire universe can come together as one, when my own country can't seem to make it happen. *And what do they see in me?* "How can I help in all of this? Why am I the one you chose as a visitor?"

Birkim, this time, answers. "We chose you because of how you think. We've seen your writings. We felt your disappointment with your country, your despair over where your world was headed. And we admired your drive to keep learning, regardless. Few people have done what you did, Ira. Instead of continuing on in life like nothing was wrong, you chose to rise up. Not only did you begin writing, but you began educating others. You took a path that is difficult and not only traveled it, but ran. You began research into subjects you didn't understand and educated yourself. You then managed to piece together information to form new thoughts and conclusions, and, even more admirable, decided to spread these new ideas to others.

"You were not the best choice, Ira, you were our only choice. Other nations have been going through what yours now is for years. We understand that. Other people in those nations have done what you do, as well. But none have gone to action as swiftly as you. It seemed as if there was little hesitation between the change in your country and your initial thoughts, and then none at all between thought and decision. Your strength of character is what brought you to the Zavilisk, and we believe it will help direct your species down the right path as well."

"But what can I do?" I question. "Surely you understand the strictness of the country I live in right now. It is illegal to ask questions. Illegal to conduct unsanctioned research. How am I supposed to call my country to action if I can't even publicly question my government's actions?"

"This is where I come in," says Birkim. "I will assist you in developing and implementing a plan. It will not be easy, Ira. I'm sure you know this. But what is it that your species says? 'When there is a will, there is a way?' Kalis and I have years of experience with this. If you can get your country to accept the idea of a universal community, living and thriving together, we can do the rest."

"You mentioned before that I am not the first visitor from Earth. Who was the first? Why are you here now when others have obviously failed?"

"There has only been one other visitor from Earth," Kalis begins. The people before us did exactly as we have with you," he continues. "They showed him our ship. They told him of our hopes for Earth. It was understood that your country was in the middle of a war at the time, but they had hoped that someone such as himself, a theoretical physicist, would be able to lead your species to accept the universal community and make the same changes we hope you can help with. They even showed him some of our technology after he asked to see how the ship was powered.

"Once he returned to Earth, though, it was soon evident that the members of the ship could not have made a worse choice. Instead of planning as he was asked, he joined the world in a very different way. He assisted in the production of the very first atomic bomb.

"As you can imagine, our ship immediately left. It was determined that your species needed to work out its issues with each other before being considered again," Birkim adds.

"We are back now," Kalis says, "Because it was our regularly scheduled time. We watched your species for over fifteen years before your country made the change that it did. *You* are here now because we believe you can fix it. Trust me, Ira. We did not choose you without considering every option. We as a species value extreme logic, remember? And we would be with you every step of the way. You will never be alone in this process."

I look to the two of them now, contemplating what to say. I do believe that our planet can be saved. I know it in my heart. I have always had faith in the world, I realize. The changes in my country made me lose sight of that. I know that there are already plans in place to eliminate pollution. There are already others calling for world peace. Through aid organizations, famine is shrinking as well. Imagine what could be done, at such an exponential rate, if the entire world was working together on these issues. We would have these problems solved in no time at all. *We* can *do this*, I think. I just don't know if I'm the one to facilitate it.

I'm an unknown on the world stage. Sure, there

are plenty of people who read my political articles. They're mostly US residents, though, not that of other countries. And my space articles haven't gathered much steam yet. One is still sitting on my computer, unfinished. And what about my family? I know my wife and kids would support me, but this is huge.

This, I realize now, is bigger than me. It's bigger than my family, or my blog. It's bigger even than my country. This is something that can change the world. Forever. This is also something that two people, more advanced than I ever thought possible, are sure that I can complete. While I have only just met them, their position makes me value their opinion. My last thought seals the deal. Bringing it back down to a personal level, I think, *imagine how this could affect my family. My kids' futures.* I shouldn't be thinking about not doing this because of them. I should be doing it for them.

My decision made, I look back into each of their eyes, a new fire raging in my heart. "You said I'll have your help?" I ask. "Because I'm going to need it. I'm also going to need some things to take back with me. If I'm going to do this, I'm going to do it in a way I know will reach the most people. And I know my species. We don't believe a thing until we see it. I need proof, or this never makes it past a joke."

"So you'll do it?" Asks Birkim, his excitement showing by the rise in his tone.

"Like you ever doubted that," I respond. "Of course, I will."

· 7 ·
The Plan
The Zavilisk, SVM-145

"TELL us what you need," says Kalis excitedly. Apparently, we're jumping right into this. *No sense in slowing down progress,* I suppose.

"Well, I'm not sure yet," I respond. "I don't know what is available to me."

"Mostly anything. Well, anything but schematics," Birkim tells me, reminding me of what happened the last time there was a visitor from Earth.

"Of course, of course," I say. "I'll need a way to communicate with you. You mentioned a communication device for speaking to the council? Is there one for communication with you as well?"

"That will not be a problem. We anticipated this, and have had our engineers working on it already," replies Kalis. "It will be ready before you leave."

"Great. Not only will it serve as a way for me to update you and seek your assistance if and when I need it, but it will also help me by allowing me to showcase some of the technologies that are out there.

"Now, what about one of the screens? The holographic panels I see everywhere. Are those portable? If I want to inspire the public, something like that would definitely do it. Now more than ever, new technology will grab and hold their attention. There is nothing like that even close to development by our species. Especially not my country."

"Yes of course. They are almost feather-light. It is just a small bar that is placed on the floor. It projects light into the air, creating the image it is programmed to show. If multiple images or videos have been programmed into it, you can choose which is displayed by swiping your hand across the image."

"Good, so I can have a video feed of the ship as well?" I ask, hoping for the best.

"I think we can do that. You would have to wait until we are in your galaxy, though. While we can make radio communication transmit throughout the universe, video doesn't work the same way. If all goes well on your end, we should be able to enter your galaxy whenever you need us."

"I can handle that," I decide. "The last thing I can think of seems fairly simple, at least, to me. I need a piece of this metal," I say, rapping my knuckles on the arm of the chair for effect. "It's another thing I can use to prove to the government that all of this is true. If I can show them that nothing like this can be found or made on Earth, it would definitely further our cause."

"Under normal circumstances, we would have to say no," begins Kalis. "But I believe this instance to be special. I think we can make an exception to the rule. I am sure we can find a piece small enough for you to return with."

"However," adds Birkim, "You must promise not to allow testing on this piece of metal, other than to determine its source, until your species is prepared to face the universe. This is our only stipulation."

"That's not a problem," I promise. *I don't even know anyone who could do any kind of tests to begin with.*

"So how do you plan to utilize these tools we provide?" Birkim asks. "I don't suppose you can travel the world and show them to every person you find."

"No, no, I can't do that. I'll have my family to think about. And I can't travel outside of the United States anyway. Even if I could, I don't have the kind of money it takes to travel like that."

"That may be something else we could help with," states Kalis slyly.

"How could you help with that?" I ask, genuinely interested.

"Our research," he begins, "is very thorough. Once we begin. We monitor everything. We know how your networks work. We can track anything, including information on your internet. Information like banking transfers. I'm sure we could move some things around."

"That's stealing!" I exclaim. "There is no way I will allow you to take money from people to support this. There has to be another way."

"Not people, my friend. Your government. We can definitely move funds from one of their accounts to yours. In fact, -"

"Hold on," I tell him. "If you have access to their networks and can move around money, can you do something else instead? Why not just create a research proposal, and then grant me permission to begin the project, seemingly coming from the office of the president. Then, you can move money from their research funding into a bank account that only I have access to, and it wouldn't catch anyone's attention. It would even open up the ability to travel internationally. They'd never realize what was happening."

"That's actually a fantastic idea. I can't think of a better way to hide this than in plain sight. You'd be able to operate and move around freely, with little to no risk of catching anyone's attention until the exact moment you want to." Birkim tells me. "Genius."

"Nah, just trying to figure out how to do this without getting thrown in jail in the process. If anyone catches on before I'm ready, I'll have to figure out how to do this *not* in plain sight." I say dryly.

"How do you intend to get the public to pay you any attention to begin with?" he asks.

"The only way to get anyone's attention these days. Social media," I say. "Once people are following what I'm doing there, I can enlist their help to move further. If I can get some believers, I can have them assist me in spreading the word. Word of mouth, more social media posts, even flyers if need be.

"Gaining the attention of someone influential would help us exponentially," I add. "If someone who has millions of social media followers, like a popular actress, for example, picks up my cause, things will speed up for sure.

"And I'll need to release information strategically as well. If I lay all my cards on the table at once, it's too easy to overlook. I need suspense. Bits and pieces will get released incrementally. Once I see that people are thirsty for more, I'll add just a little more information to the pile. Keeping the public's interest is probably the most important part of all of this." I say.

"Why is that?" Kalis asks. "I would have thought to get your government's interest would be the most important part."

"Because," I begin, "When the entire nation is calling for change, or begging for a response to the mysterious aliens, the government will have no choice but to play ball. They'll have to do something. And they can't arrest everyone in the country. Sure, I may have to play it safe and lay low until they're ready to work with me. But at that point, I think arresting me would be the worst possible thing they could do. To the public, this would just look like guilt. Everyone would immediately be convinced that I was right. Even the doubters would see this as a sign that the government is covering something up.

"If worst comes to worst, I can use my travel abilities to leave the US and stay in another country for the duration. I'm sure I could find refuge somewhere else for a while if I needed to," I finish.

"This is all just for your country, though," says Birkim. "How do you intend to reach the world?"

"Well, I will be able to travel if I get a research grant. But I'd like for the people in other countries to be prepped before I get there. Open minds will definitely help. What are the chances you can unblock my IP address? Enable my social media accounts to reach outside of the United States?"

"We can do even better than that," Kalis says. "Once we're in your galaxy, we would be able to route all of your network traffic through our ship, and then broadcast it back to Earth that way. Not only could you reach the rest of the world, but you'd also be able to do it without your government ever realizing you're accessing the internet at all."

"That's perfect! Better than perfect. Once I've got the people in the US pushing our government for a response, I can move onto the world. I'd use the same technique as I did in my country, but add in videos and pictures of what's currently happening in the US Show them the social media accounts of people in my country. Lead them into the belief that everyone in the US is already on board. I think it would speed the process up in the rest of the world.

"Then," I add, "All I have to do is tell the world

that the only course of action left is to gather our world leaders and convince them to speak with me and then, eventually, the council. I know the people of Earth. If our world leaders say no to that conversation when the entire world is rallying for them to have it, there would be hell to pay. Just like you said, our people can rally together behind a common goal. This would be one of them whether the council is contacted or not. The leaders of these countries know that the fallout would be astronomical if they turned their back on the world's population. There would be anarchy. While it sounds terrible, they would never allow it to happen.

"In the end, I believe that seeing the public rally together over something like this would only convince them further that we, as a species, are ready for the next step. Just like it has already convinced you," I say, motivating myself as I finish.

"Ira, you continue to remind me why we chose you for this task. Your critical thinking rivals ours, and that says a lot. I do believe you are perfectly prepared to do this, whether you think so or not." Birkim says, a genuine smile on his face.

"There is one other thing I'd like for you to take with you. If you're going to give them examples of 'alien' life, then I say we go all the way with it. Let me send an example of a non-carbon based life form with you when you go," Kalis tells me.

"Wait. What?" After all the time we spent going over the ship and any questions I had, I forgot his previous comment about carbon based life. "What other types of life are there?"

"Well," Kalis begins, "the most prevalent form, other than carbon based, is silicon based. There are others as well, like sulfur based. The only viable form is silicon, though. The only reason it is able to survive is because of its unique ability to withstand the cold.

"Silicon based life forms don't generally inhabit planets, and they are never advanced like you or I. They are usually the size of insects, and swarm the same way. But they swarm in space. They can't really cause any damage. They just feed off of particles on asteroids or space junk they come across. Most regard them as insignificant.

"I only mention them now," he continues, "because I think you should show your world that not only does life exist elsewhere in the universe, but multiple *kinds* of life exist as well. This will only serve to bolster their opinion that the future really could lie with the universal community. Of course, it wouldn't hurt that the idea of numerous forms of life exist comes on the heels of finding out that other life exists period. The intrigue this would cause speaks for itself."

"I see," I say, hesitant. "There really is no danger?"

"None." He assures me. "They are basically irrelevant in the universe."

"Okay then. We'll add them to my inventory."

"Well, I think that does it for planning. Should we retire for the evening? If there is nothing else, I think we should set this into motion tomorrow," Birkim says.

"Fine with me. I'd really love to get back to my family."

"Oh, I am sure you are ready for that," Birkim adds. "And I'm sure they are ready as well."

Standing, we begin to walk through the viewing room. "Would you like to see a specimen first?" asks Kalis. "There is one on a table on the way out of this room."

Nodding, I fall in line behind Kalis as we weave through rows of tables. Most of the things here I recognize now from the daily trip into and out of the room. As we stop, I realize we're standing in front of a table of white canisters.

Picking one up, he holds his finger over a small grey patch, unnoticed before amid all the white. When he does this, the lid rotates off, as if on a small hinge controlled by a motor.

Reaching inside, he pulls out a smaller cylindrical glass jar. It has the same white metal on the top and bottom, sealng the glass tube shut. Inside is a tiny creature. It can only be described as ugly. It is all black, with spider-like legs and wings that resemble a fighter jet, angled back and triangular in shape. It is segmented, broken up into two distinct sections, the wings beginning near the head and ending where the first segment meets the second. The entire thing has a rubbery appearance and is no longer than two inches.

"This is it?" I ask. "Is it dead? You said it's safe, right?"

"Yes of course," Kalis replies. "It would never

have been brought aboard this ship alive, if though it is safe. It can even be removed from this jar when the time comes. It has been sterilized, so it poses no risk to your people." He shows me how to remove it, and how to work the metal outer container, before putting it all back together and placing it on the table.

We continue the walk back to my room, talking about tomorrow. "So I will leave tomorrow then?" I ask.

"Yes. As soon as we have everything ready, we'll take you back to the isolation room. It will be much easier to get home, and a lot less painful. Since you are on our ship already, the amount of energy needed can be increased during the process instead of hitting you with it all at once. You'll still see the energy ball, of course. It just won't feel like you're being electrocuted."

"Well that makes me feel a little better," I say. "I definitely was not looking forward to that again. As long as I expect it, I think I'll be fine."

Reaching my room, the door opens for me, ready to receive me for one more night. "Goodnight," I tell Kalis. "I'll be ready to go in the morning."

"Goodnight, Ira. We'll be ready as well."

I turn from my door, sad and excited both to see the next day come. While I am more than ready to see my family, I know I will miss the friends I've made aboard the ship. I hear it shut behind me as I sit on the bed, exhausted. I know as soon as I lay my head on the pillow, I'll crash. Just like before, I replay the events of the day in my head, while I get comfortable. It's so much, I don't think I can get through it all before I sleep. I can't focus on that anyway, I realize. I'll finally see my wife and children tomorrow. With that, I fall into what must be the deepest sleep of my life.

•8•
The Gift
The Zavilisk, SVM-145

WAKING up, I stretch under the comforter for a second before the realization of what happens today hits me. Jumping out of bed, I throw on the clothes that I arrived in, surprisingly happy about putting on clothes that haven't been washed in so long. Checking my appearance in the mirror again, I decide I look like a caveman. *Oh well*, I think. *I'm going home.* As I emerge from the bathroom, the door opens as expected.

"Good morning, Ira," says the Captain. "I wanted to come down and join you three today, since it is the last time I will see you. How are you feeling?"

"Nervous. Excited. Everything in between. It's a mix," I laugh. "I'm confident that the people of Earth can come together as one. I'm less sure about me being able to get them there."

"Just keep up the confidence and resolve we've seen in you so far," he says, ushering me into the hallway. We begin walking. "You'll do just fine."

"Easy for you to say when you're watching from way up here."

"No, it's not easy for us at all, Ira. We all want the same thing. To bring another planet into the community. The last thing we ever want to do is leave, knowing it will be at least fifty more years before someone even studies them again. We'd much rather see a species succeed instead of struggle."

"I understand that," I tell him, feeling foolish for saying what I did. If they didn't care, they wouldn't be out here, scouting the universe and helping species achieve greatness.

"Can I give you one more little incentive before you go?" He asks, leading me to an answer we both know I will give.

"Of course," I reply, nodding. "I'll take all the motivation I can get."

"Do you remember the things I said I was prevented from telling you? There were a few of them, if I am not mistaken."

"I do."

"Well, when you succeed, and I do mean *when*, I will personally tell you those things. Once your world agrees to join the community, I won't be obligated to keep them as secrets any longer. I think you deserve as much. If I could do more, I would."

"Thank you, Alter," I say, sincerely. While calm on the outside, on the inside I'm reeling again at the idea of learning more about the universe we live in. He was right, of course. This is definitely added motivation.

Entering the viewing room, I realize this is my last time to see this magnificent view. It's still hard to fathom that so much nothing is actually everything. Hopefully, it'll get easier. Hopefully, I'll have the chance to make it easier for *everyone.*

We reach the window, and I stare out. The feeling of vertigo doesn't come anymore. It has been replaced with joy, even excitement. I can't help but consider the future each time I stare out this window at the great darkness beyond.

Without my knowing it, Kalis and Birkim have silently approached from behind me. They each slide to my left side, now all four of us standing in a line, each looking out over the top of the ship, into space.

"It never loses its beauty, does it?" Asks Birkim.

"It really doesn't," I respond. "But you know what else doesn't either?"

"What?" he asks, a look of intrigue on his face. Kalis and Alter now face me as well.

"My family," I say. "My amazing, difficult, perfect family." I pause, looking back out the window for a moment. "I think I am ready to go be with them. I'm going to need their support for what's to come, and it will take some time to explain where I've been first."

"Well, before you go, there is something we'd like

to give you," Kalis says, bringing his hands around from behind his back. Holding them up, I can see that is it a small clear box. It's only about three inches square and looks to be solid glass, save for a speck of grey inside.

"What is it?" I ask, leaning in for a closer look.

Extending his hand in front of him, gesturing for me to take the box, Kalis tells me, "It is yours, Ira. Your little piece of the universe, in case this does not turn out the way we hope. Inside of this glass box are a few small particles of dust. This dust, my friend, is from the center of the universe. It is the oldest space dust you could ever find. It has been stored on this ship for a very long time, but we decided last night that it is time for us to pass it on. We can think of no one better to have it."

I pull it in closer, bringing it up to my eyes. Sure enough, I can see the dust clearly now. Looking closer, I realize that the dust has a faint glow to it, almost like the rooms of the ship. *Will it always glow like this, or is it just the ship?* I ask to myself. I'm struck by the significance of this gift. I am the first, and maybe the only, human to ever see or hold anything like this. These few specks of dust, older than most can even understand. Their weightlessness is deceiving. They hold the weight of the universe, billions of years in the making.

"I'm sure you know after your studies, that the English language does not have a strong enough word for me to use to show my gratitude right now. But I can express it through actions. I will make sure you know, without a shadow of a doubt, that I have earned this amazing gift. Thank you."

"You are quite welcome," says Birkim. "Thank us by joining us in the community soon. We have all the confidence that you will earn that gift and more, Ira. We know you can do it."

"Well, if that is all, I suppose we should prepare you for your trip back," the Captain tells me. "We have everything ready for you in the isolation room."

Before I turn to go, I take one last look at the space beyond the window. I'm going to miss being able to look out and see nothing but calm, empty nothingness. In the same way, though, I already miss the chaos of home. Turning away, I begin my last long walk aboard this amazing ship.

During the trip, there is little conversation. It could be respect, as we all share the knowledge that these are my last few minutes aboard the Zavilisk. Or it could be sadness, all recognizing the fact that this could be the last time we see each other. Regardless of the reason, it is eerily quiet in these corridors today.

"Did they talk to you about your trip back?" asks Alter. "I know there isn't much they can say."

"They did. I know it's a safe process. And it won't last as long or be as painful this time. Now that I know what it is, though, I think I could keep calm, and it wouldn't be nearly as painful anyways."

"You never cease to amaze me, Ira," Birkim interjects. "The process won't really change all that much this time, to be completely honest. The distance will be the same. That is what dictates the amount of energy needed to make the transfer. But usually those that are prepared for it fare much better, they just don't know it. You, on the other hand, have figured it out already."

"There is one thing about humans that you haven't quite figured out yet," I tell him. "As much as you can study, read our pasts in books and on computers, and recognize our body language, you can never know everything that is going on in our brains. We are fairly predictable that way. On Earth, we use polygraph machines is much the same way you can just read us. There are plenty of people that can beat those machines. Don't always trust us to give a 'tell' of what our thoughts are, and never underestimate what we are capable of."

"Ira we have easily learned as much from being with you these past few days as we have from all of our studies before. And that is one thing we have always known about humans. We know better than to underestimate you."

With that, we reach the final turn of the halls. I can see the open doors leading through the gas chamber, to the isolation room. I slow a bit, taking in this last bit with respect now, instead of the original fear. We pass through the gas chamber and I look around in awe at what these people are capable of. What we could be capable of, if we can get ourselves together.

As we step into the isolation room, I see a bag

on the floor in the center of the room. It is the same strange multipurpose linen they wear and use for everything else, green in color. I pick it up and look inside. Everything I requested is here. I can see the tube used to project the hologram screen and the canister with the silicon based life form inside. There is also a square of metal, about four inches by four inches, smooth and white and shiny, reflecting light back at me from inside the bag.

I gently place my particle block in the bag as I pull out what must be the communication device. It looks like a block of metal, no bigger than the average cell phone. There is no antennae, and no buttons that I can see. It is the same shiny metal like that in the viewing and other common rooms. Lifting it into everyone's view, I ask the obvious question. "How does it work?"

Smiling, Kalis says "you've already made it work, Ira. All you have to do is hold it in your hand and speak. We will always hear."

"Yeah, we definitely need technology like this on Earth," I say, grinning back. "Thank you again. For everything."

"It is no problem," Alter says. "We look forward to hearing from you soon."

"Take care," Birkim tells me, looking into my eyes and showing more emotion than I've ever seen from him.

Kalis walks over to me. Lifting his hand, he takes mine and shakes. This simple gesture means so much, showing how serious they all are about integrating us into their culture and community. "Take care, my friend. And good luck."

With that, they all step from the isolation room, the door shutting behind them. My mixed emotions get the better of me again, and I feel a tear slip from my eye. *I have got to quit doing this so much,* I tell myself. Entirely too much crying lately.

Remembering how it went when I was first brought here, I take a seat on the floor against the back wall of the room. Almost immediately, I see the ball of electricity. It starts in the center of the room, slowly expanding outwards. It feels much calmer this time, without the vibrations and wind. I was expecting each of those to occur first, and had prepared myself accordingly. The bag is tucked tight between my back and the wall, and I made sure there was nothing that could work loose from my pockets. *Just happens when they're bringing me to the ship, maybe?*

I stare, studying it this time since I know not to fear it. The way it grows, spreading and spreading, is mesmerizing. I can feel it now, like last time. It electrifies everything in the room. My hair stands on end. I can see small arcs jumping from the hovering mass to strike the wall, seeking out the metal that electricity so desires. The brightness grows with its size, quickly overtaking my ability to endure it. I finally have to look away.

Closing my eyes, I put my head between my knees, my thighs pulled up to my chest, and try to remain calm. I do not fear the process anymore. I am trying to contain my excitement. Excitement at knowing what's coming, and at traveling such an amazing distance again, all within the blink of an eye.

Finally, I feel it take over. *Thank God.* My anticipation alone my kill me before I get home. The electricity reaches me, tapping me with the small arcs flying off from the center. I know it's coming any second. Bracing myself, I feel at peace.

And finally, it engulfs me.

Schzwack! Again, the mass of a train, crushing me.

I'm going home.

Part
2
Progress

*The contemplation of celestial things will make
a man both speak and think more sublimely and
magnificently when he descends to human affairs.*
— *Marcus Tullius Cicero, c. 30 BCE*

· 9 ·
Home
Charlottesville, VA

HOME at last.

I slowly open my eyes as I wake up, taking in my surroundings. The room is filled with natural sunlight, and I find comfort in this, not realizing how much I missed it. The beige carpet feels soft beneath me. Sitting up, I realize everything seems to be back to normal. The mantel is filled with framed photographs and trinkets. Pictures are hung on the walls. The kids' toys are put away neatly, a rare sight with toddlers.

As I scan the room, the thoughts hit me. *Did I dream this? Was any of it real?* Then I notice the proof I need, for myself now and for the world. The green linen bag leans against the couch, almost as if it belongs here.

I stand up and walk towards it, eager to make sure everything is intact and here. Opening it up, the past four days rush back to me at once. Kalis, Birkim, and Alter. The ship, the Zavilisk. The beautiful space that surrounded us, seemingly void of everything except the twinkles in the distance.

Everything is there. The holographic screen, radio, canister, and square of metal, all as it should be. And resting on top of it all, my prized possession, the glass block of space dust from the center of the universe.

Satisfied that I have what I need, I sit the bag on the couch. Wondering where my family is, I set off down the hallway, grazing my fingers against the wall as if still trying to make sure it's real. I take in the pictures with a renewed sense of purpose, needing to find the faces looking back at me.

The office door is open, with no one inside. The computer and extra monitor are off, and the room looks recently cleaned. Everything is where it belongs.

The door to the kids' room is open as well. Leaning in, there are no children in sight. The beds look like they haven't been slept in for days, there's no laundry in sight, and the toys are put away here too. *Where are they?* I wonder.

Across the hall, our bedroom door is closed. Opening it, I immediately look toward Brynn's side of the bed.

There's a lump.

The lump moves.

"Ira?" Brynn says groggily. Completely awake now, her eyes widen. "Ira!" she yells, sitting up just as I get to her side.

Cradling her head against my chest, I tell her, "I'm here baby. I'm home. I'm so sorry Brynn."

"We didn't know what happened," she sobs, the tears flowing onto my shirt. "The police are looking for you. I filed a missing person report! I sent the kids to their grandparent's house. We got home and you were gone and the house was a wreck and I was so scared," she rambles, pressing her head even tighter into me.

"I know, Brynn. I know," I whisper, pulling her head into my hands. I look into her eyes and tell her, "I love you, Brynn."

"I love you too, Ira," she responds as we kiss. It feels like the first. The fireworks and butterflies, impossibly mixed together inside me, take over like I'm a kid again.

I climb across her and lay down in the middle of the bed, pulling her down with me. She rests her head on my chest as she mumbles that she missed me. Wiping her eyes and cheeks, she looks up to me.

"Where have you been?" she asks. She doesn't sound accusatory. Just inquisitive, honestly wondering what in the world happened.

"Please just lay with me a minute?" I ask her, almost pleading. "I've missed you. I promise I will explain everything. First, though, I want to just enjoy your company for a minute. I have had the longest four days of my life."

Nodding, she lays her head back down onto my chest. I hold her there, one hand on the back of her head, my fingers interlaced with her hair. The other rests on her side, slowly sliding up and down as I do everything I can to comfort her.

I close my eyes, but don't allow myself to nod off. I missed this. Resting together, curling up in bed just to talk or sleep. I knew I would be happy to be home, but I didn't realize quite how much I needed this.

"Okay babe. We gotta get up or I'm gonna fall asleep," I tell her, regretting the need to stay awake. I'd do anything to fall asleep with her right now.

She sits up, and we head back down the hallway. We turn into the kitchen and start a pot of coffee. As it brews, I grab the pack of cigarettes on the counter and head for the door. "Come with me?" I ask, hoping she will.

Heading my way, she kisses me again and walks toward the door. We step outside into the fresh spring air and sit on the step, Brynn immediately leaning her head onto my shoulder. As I smoke, I take everything in again. "I missed this," I begin. "The grass, the trees, the birds, and flowers. There wasn't any of this where I was." And it's true. If I enjoyed it all before, I love it now.

Kissing her forehead, I stand up. We head back into the kitchen, each making a cup of coffee. I take a sip, not caring about the heat. It's as if I can make up for lost time by doing everything I used to do before I took the trip of a lifetime.

We sit on the couch, and I make sure to take the side nearest my bag. The last thing I need is for Brynn to open it and see the contents without first getting an explanation from me. *I do need to quit stalling, though,* I tell myself. *Just do it.* I know I don't have a choice but to tell her. But, I realize now, the hardest part is telling a family member. Telling anyone else will be easy compared to convincing Brynn I'm not a lying lunatic. There is one thing in the bag I may be able to use, though.

Reaching in, I pull out the radio they made for me to communicate with them. Looking to Brynn, I say, "Brynn, I don't know how to tell you where I've been. It's unbelievable. And I know that no matter how much you trust me, this would be hard for you to believe without something more."

Holding it out in front of us both, I tell her, "So here it is. Something more."

"What is it?" Brynn asks. To her, all it must look like is a block of metal.

"It is a radio. It was made for me by the people that brought me onto their ship. They took me into space, Brynn."

She looks at me, trying to read my face for a joke or lie. "You can't be serious. Don't joke with me, Ira. You were just gone for four days. This is ridiculous."

"I am serious, and I'll prove it to you," I tell her. Hoping it works just as they explained it would, I speak. "Kalis? Are you there?"

A few seconds pass, and then, "I am here, my friend. Though I wasn't expecting to hear from you, quite this soon."

Brynn's eyes widen. "I wasn't really expecting it either," I say. "But this was the easiest way to explain it to Brynn."

"Aah, this is understandable. Brynn, it is nice to meet you. Your husband spoke highly of you while he was here with us."

"Who are you?" Brynn asks. "Ira tells me you're in space? What, like an astronaut, right?"

"No, Brynn. Not quite. I am Kalis, and I am the chief scientific officer aboard our ship, the Zavilisk. As you husband told you, we are in space. But not your galaxy, or any galaxy nearby. We are currently in galaxy SVM-145 in the Shapley supercluster. Did your husband tell you where that is when he was writing his article?"

"He did," Brynn responds. She grips my hand and squeezes. "But... how did he get there?"

"That is something that he does not even know yet, Brynn. But he will, and then I am sure he will tell you. If it helps, I think there is something else that he has that may help you believe further.

"Ira," he says, speaking to me now. "Perhaps you should show her the gift we gave you."

I'm already reaching inside the bag as he says this, pulling the block from the safety of the green linen. I place it in Brynn's hands. "Hold it close and look inside," I tell her.

She does, and I can see her eyes growing wide again. "What is it?" she asks.

"It's dust, Brynn. From the middle of the universe.

Here, look," I say as I jump from the couch. I close the blinds, darkening the room. Sure enough, I can see it.

"Is it glowing?!" she asks, incredulously.

"It is," Kalis says. "It's quite beautiful, really. We thought it would be a nice gift for Ira. A token of our gratitude."

"Is there anything else you need?" he asks. "If so, I am sure we would be able to get it to you with time."

"No, I don't think so. Not right now, at least. Have you done everything here that I asked?"

"It has all been taken care of. Brynn, it was nice meeting you. Ira, I hope to hear from you again soon, my friend."

"You too, Kalis. And you will." I say.

"Goodbye," Brynn stammers, still staring into the block.

I put the radio away and turn to Brynn.

"You're serious," she says. "You were in space. With *aliens.*"

"Well, technically," I reply, using Alter's comment, "I was the alien. But yes. I was."

"What was it like?"

"It was beautiful. Like nothing you could ever even imagine. And the ship was amazing. Technology that could never even be dreamed of on Earth." I launch into detail, telling her all about the ship, every single thing I can think of coming out in a rush. I tell her about how I got there as well. I describe the other people I met, and how they treated me as an equal, not as an experiment like you hear in made up reports and movies. I pull the items I brought with me from the bag and show them to her as I describe them.

She is especially interested in the light and asks me to describe it further, which I do with pleasure. She doesn't like the silicon-based life form, but I assure her that it is harmless and dead. She seems satisfied with that.

Finally, she asks the question that I knew was coming. She looks up at me, pulling her eyes away from the piece of metal in her hand. "As amazing as it is Ira, I still don't understand something. Why? Why you, of all the people on Earth? What could they have possibly wanted?"

"That, sweetheart, is even harder to believe than me being there at all," I say, with all the sincerity in the world.

"The number of inhabited planets I predicted was low. Extremely low. And the number of those that have advanced life are higher than I could have ever imagined. There is a universal community. All of the advanced species take part. They don't war, or destroy the planets they inhabit.

"They also keep track of other species in the universe that aren't as advanced as they are, but are getting close. There is a council that studies them. When they think the species is ready, they make contact.

"They were only a few years from making contact with Earth, before our president took office and made the changes he made. Because of the global scale of those changes, they decided we weren't ready. However, they talked with the council, and due to a trait that we have, something rare in the universe, they decided to take more direct action."

"Direct action? Like what?" Brynn asks.

"Like me," I respond. "They brought me on board and taught me everything I've told you. They want me to stage a kind of intervention. For the planet. If it works, the council will take us in."

"But what happens when they take us in? It's not like we can travel like they can. Does it really matter?"

"It matters greatly. Because if we do join the community, we will have access to every bit of technology they have. We would become equals with the rest of the universe. It would end the need for discrimination, war, everything. It's the most important event that could ever take place for the human race."

"Well, what do we need to do? Like as a planet, what needs to happen?"

"Well, the biggest thing we need to do is just get the world leaders to speak to the council and pledge their commitment to a few things. Ending famine, ending war, and ending pollution."

"Oh Jesus, there's no way we could get anyone to do that, Ira. You know that."

"I used to think that. But with this," I hold up the bag, "I believe all that changes. I think if the people of the world see that there is more to life than just living, more than just Earth, I think we stand a chance of making real change."

"I don't know, hun. That's a tall order. You really think you can get people like our current president to go along with that?"

"I don't think it matters babe. Once the rest of the world is calling on our leaders to do this, they would be idiots not to do it, whether they want to or not. And I think they'd be overthrown if they tried to go against it."

"You might be right, I guess. So what's your plan?"

"It's pretty straightforward, actually. I want to start with social media. Once I get a presence there, I think everything else will fall into place.

"The first thing we need to do, though, is tell the police to call off the search. The last thing I need right now is for anyone to think there's anything weird going on. At least, until I tell them there is something weird going on.

"And then, we need to get the kids. I'm dying to see them. Hopefully, your parents haven't filled them with too much worry."

"Okay, you're right. I'll tell the police you went on a fishing trip I had forgotten about or something."

Brynn made her phone calls. The police asked to speak to me, and after they had confirmed I was myself, they released the case. She went on to call her parents and confirmed that the kids barely asked about me while I've been gone. She told them that I was home, but that we couldn't tell them what is going on. They didn't like it, but said they'll be by with the girls soon.

While we begin getting the house ready for two hyper toddlers, I fill Brynn in on my plan for the next few days. She agrees that it seems like the best we can do for now.

"There are some things about it that I don't like," she tells me, "but I don't think we have many other options."

"I know," I tell her. "I have my concerns as well. But we're resourceful. We'll make it happen."

We continue talking, sealing the plan on what to do when her parents get here. We're both sure that they'll ask more questions, and Brynn decided we need to get our stories straight.

With that finished, we finally relax on the couch. As much as we can, anyway. The days ahead loom over us like a cloud. I just can't figure out if it's white and puffy like those on a summer afternoon, or grey, filled with a storm.

· 10 ·
Shots Fired
Charlottesville, Virginia

THE next morning, I wake up with a smile. The night before was perfect. I was relieved when Brynn's parents didn't question us further on my disappearance, though we were prepared for pretty much any question. Seeing the kids again was completely uneventful. Like any other toddler, they couldn't care less that I was gone. They were just glad that I was home to play.

The rest of the night was great as well. Not because there was anything special, but because it was normal. Brynn and I decided early in the evening to keep everything the same. We don't want the kids to know that anything is different until we have no other choice but to tell them.

As we sip our coffee, I explain to Brynn exactly

what I want to do today. After she agrees, she surprises me. "I'm going to call work and ask for some time off," she says. "If you're really going to go all in on this, I want to be right there with you. I have a feeling you're going to need the support."

"Fine with me," I tell her. I'd love nothing more than to spend every possible minute with her. "I'm sure I'll need to pick your brain occasionally."

When the kids wake up, we play for a bit before Brynn's parents come back. They agreed to take them for the weekend, so Brynn and I could "work on something." I get hugs and kisses as they leave, somehow making their absence harder and easier at the same time.

Without putting it off any longer, I get to work. The first thing I do is take pictures of the items I have from the ship. Up close and far away, with and without a ruler. I take pictures of the bar and then of the holographic screen. I make sure to catch the light emitted from the glass block with dust. I use different angles for the metal, catching the way it reflects light and its thickness. I even open the canister and get a few close-ups of the weird space bug inside. My attempt at proof that they're not just digitally produced photographs, I have Brynn take pictures of me holding each item as well.

After that, I set up a new email address. It doesn't have my name or anything identifiable because it doesn't need to. I want to keep my personal information as safe as possible for now, though I know there will come a time when everyone that I'm close to knows that I am the owner. That is, if all goes according to the plan.

Next, I go through my personal social media accounts and set them all to private. I don't want anyone to be able to put two and two together, and somehow link my new accounts to those in my name. Then I begin creating new accounts with all of the major social networks. I use a different name for them all, and add my new email in the contact information, just to use for the campaign I am about to embark on.

Now the real work begins. Crafting the message. I need each account to provide the same basic message, but I know I'll need to tailor it to each account I use. I brainstorm with Brynn for a while, bouncing ideas back and forth. It's only been a few hours, and I already realize this is harder than I thought it would be. *If this is hard, the rest is going to be awful,* I think.

The first social network is the hardest. Before making the first post on my fresh account, I have to add friends. I seek out popular people that I can add as friends instead of just follow. Going through their friends, I add anyone that has a lot of friends. I don't need to know them. I just need my posts to pop up on their news feed. Hopefully, I can get a few shares that way and really get the ball rolling. For the message, I decide to post:

"I have proof of the existence of aliens. No joke. Like and share enough, and I will start posting it. I want everyone to see. Stay tuned."

Not wanting to lose my nerve, I jam the Enter key and don't look back. "So it begins," I think out loud.

Next, I head to my other account. This one is easier. I follow a bunch of people who immediately follow me back. Everyone knows how it works here. *You scratch my back, I'll scratch yours.* Everyone follows each other to increase their numbers. With that done, I type out my message. Using '#Aliens,' I write,

"Aliens are real. I can prove it. Share and follow, and I'll add pictures. Get more people to follow if you want more."

Hitting Enter again, I sit back in the chair. *I sure hope this works.*

Closing both tabs of my browser, I open up the search window. The first person I look for is the last CEO of SETI. I then find the last Director of NASA. The last person I search for is the Astronomy Professor at UCLA, currently the leading Professor in the field. I copy all of their emails into my notes, then open up my new email account.

This message needs to have much more depth. These aren't popular college kids I'm trying to use. They are the top scientists in their field. To them, I write:

"Hello, Gentleman. I am writing you all

today to tell you of an amazing discovery. I have irrefutable evidence that advanced life exists throughout the universe. I understand that this is hard to believe. But I also know what is at stake by even starting this conversation with you. All I ask of you is that you keep this communication between the four of us for now. You are the only people I have contacted regarding this, and will remain so until the time comes. If I get a response, I will reveal everything that I have. I know that I am an unknown to you, but give this a chance. I have the possibility to change the world. I'll leave you with a question. Why would I tell you this, something so easily faked, when our country is in a place where none of this would normally matter anymore?"

Copying their email addresses into the 'To' and 'Carbon Copy' sections, I send the message.

Now, all I can do is wait. The anticipation is eating at me already. I know it will soon feel like a wild animal inside of me, carving its way out. The worst part is the unknown. If this doesn't work, the rest of the plan is at risk as well. And there is so much that could easily go wrong. While I have tried to plan for every contingency, I learned early in life that every plan is worthless after the first shot is fired. And now, after I've made my first post and sent my first email, "Shots fired." I say. "Shots fired."

With the list for today complete already, Brynn

and I decide to go out for lunch. With everything that's happening, I have a feeling this will be the last time either of us gets to enjoy being out without being recognized or worse. We go for Italian, which both of us love, and fill up on pasta.

Arriving home, I check my social media accounts, and nearly have a heart attack. I have hundreds of messages already, and tons of friend requests. There are already more followers on my new accounts than I have on the accounts in my real name. It's unbelievable.

I spend the next two hours doing the most monotonous task I've ever done in my life. Accepting friend requests took two hours of my life away that I'll never get back, and I am not happy about it. I fear the morning, when hundreds could turn into thousands.

The messages are a mix. I have some that are great. People wish me luck, tell me how excited they are to see what I have, and acknowledge the craziness of what I just did in public. Others are rude, calling me every name in the book, and telling me that I am a fake or calling me an idiot for saying something like this on social media. I decide to make up a generic response and reply to every message, kind and rude both. "Thank you for your interest and support of this cause. Evidence will be available shortly," I tell them all. I want to gain as much social media attention as I can before I release anything.

When I check my email, I see that both the ex SETI CEO and ex-Director of NASA have already emailed me back. They both basically have the same message in response: "Thanks for emailing me, I am very interested, and I understand that no one would lie about something like this anymore, because there is no point, since research cannot be done. However, I still need proof to really believe anything." There was more to each email, but that was the basic structure of each. I decide to give the professor more time before I respond to anyone. I want him to be included, and once I get the ball rolling faster I don't know that I'll have time to respond to individual emails.

Brynn sits with me the entire time, giving a commentary of what I am reading. She definitely helps lighten the mood, and I need it while dealing with the social media circus I have gotten myself into.

With that done, I decide to act on a hunch. I spend the next few hours researching senators who opposed the president. From there, I narrowed it down to those who opposed the wall and everything else that came with it. I then rank them, in order of their will to fight. Some fought hard, right up until the end, while others gave in rather early. I write down their names and emails in a list and save it on paper and on my computer. I may need these for later.

As Brynn and I eat a late dinner, we run through the plan once more. It's already moving much faster than either of us predicted, so we had to make a few small changes, mainly the timeline. "I still can't believe how quickly people caught on!" Brynn says.

"I can't either, really. I was expecting it to get hectic, but I always thought it would take a few days.

I guess this is what I get for assuming."

"I can't believe how rude some of those people were," Brynn adds, irritated. "There's no need to act like that."

"I know babe. But really, I don't care. Any attention is good attention right now, I think. The fact that some people don't believe is a good thing right now. Because when I present evidence, and the people I emailed back me up, it's going to look even more legitimate. They'll come around. People tend to just follow the popular opinion anymore."

We finish eating, and Brynn cleans up as I check my email. Finally, I see that the professor has emailed me back. He sent basically the same message as the other two did, but offered up the equipment of his university to verify any physical evidence I may provide."

I respond back to all three of them in one email again.

"Thank you for responding back so quickly. I appreciate your realization that time is of the essence. Your verification of these items will prove essential to my overall plan. Unfortunately, at this time, I am not able to reveal this plan to you yet. You will find out when the rest of the United States does. Trust me when I say it is worth it. Please remember, discretion is immensely important right now. I am trusting the three of you to do the right thing. Professor, I am unable to get any of these items to you for testing right now, but when the time is right I will make sure you are the one to have the honors. I know that you each have been greatly affected by the president shutting down your programs and research. This is our chance to make the world right again. I have attached pictures of the evidence I have in my possession. I hope your jaws don't hit the floor too hard. Have a good night gentleman, and I look forward to hearing from you soon."

I pick the best pictures to attach, making sure each one is matched with a picture that contains measurements, as well as one of me holding each item. I click send and look over at Brynn, who took a seat beside me a while ago.

"Hell of a day, right?" I ask.

"It sure was," she replies. "What now?"

"I need to accept more friend requests. Then I think we should hit the sack."

"Sounds good to me," Brynn says. "Just watching you has worn me out today."

I give her a kiss before turning back to the computer. I check on the picture sharing social network first, but I know it can pretty much run itself. Sure enough, I have more followers already. I choose not to respond to any personal messages here. Not many people use the feature anyway. Opening up the first social network, I see that I have plenty more requests to accept. I click away as Brynn leans into me and reads a book. I glance over and notice it's one of my old books about space, soft and worn around the edges from decades of use.

"Studying?" I joke.

"Sure," she answers. "Though I don't know that this book will really do space any justice anymore, from what you've told me."

"No, I really don't think it will. But enjoy it. You can tell me how much of it is wrong when all of this is behind us."

I finish up accepting the requests and shut down the computer. We walk the dog one more time, enjoying the cool night air. Brynn is looking up, studying the sky, and I can tell exactly what she's thinking.

"Trying to picture what it was like?"

"Yeah," she begins. "I just can't imagine. Seeing a sky full of nothing but galaxies instead of stars. I don't think beautiful is strong enough of a word to describe what I'm imagining."

"Well, if what you're imagining is anything close to what I saw, then you're exactly right. There *is* no word to describe it. And I can guarantee you, your imagination is nothing compared to what it's really like."

We head inside and get ready for bed. After kissing me goodnight, Brynn rolls onto her side and scoots in next to me, her back to my chest. I drape my arm over her and kiss her head before closing my eyes.

"Let's get some rest," I say.

"We're gonna have a busy day tomorrow, I think," she replies. "I love you."

"I love you too, Brynn."

Closing my eyes, I picture the view I had from the Zavilisk, ever hopeful that I'll see it again one day. And I know that if that day comes, I'll have my amazing wife, and hopefully my kids, with me as well. *Now that's a sight that's indescribable,* I think as I fall asleep.

·11·
Change
Charlottesville, Virginia

THE next morning, we grab our coffee, call the kids, and get down to business. The first thing I do is check my email while Brynn logs on to my new social media accounts. I have fresh emails from the scientists I've been in contact with. They've all agreed to support me, so long as they are the first to have the option of studying the items I have. I agree and respond, telling them to be prepared to catch a flight and thanking them again for their continued help and support.

Putting my computer aside, Brynn slides hers onto my lap. I choose which social network to open first, and see that support has grown even more. My original message has been reposted thousands of times. The overall consensus is good, with excitement growing much higher than resentment now. I also have entirely too many new followers to count.

Deciding now is a good time to further my plan, I post a picture of me standing next to the holographic screen. "I promised a picture," I add to the message before pressing enter.

"Let's see how much attention that gets," I tell Brynn.

Next, I check on the other account. I have just as many friend requests on this one as I do followers on the other, now. I get to work accepting them all while Brynn and I talk.

"How do you think it's going so far?" she asks.

"I think it's going just like I had hoped it would," I say. "It actually makes me a little nervous. The social media accounts are doing well, and the scientists are interested. It's going great. I just feel like it'll all come crashing down soon. Nothing ever goes this perfectly."

"God I hope not. I'm keeping my fingers crossed that everything goes exactly as you've planned," Brynn replies. "The easier, the better."

We keep talking as I spend another two hours accepting friend requests. I'm getting tired of this part. Finally finished, I post another picture. This time, I choose the canister with the weird life form, adding the same message to another account. I also link the two, so they can see that picture as well. I then go back and forth, adding pictures and typing messages, linking them all together like a chain. If someone sees one, they can see them all.

By the time I'm finished, it's lunch time. We eat while we watch the federally sanctioned news. Nothing but the usual. Apparently, it's all rainbows and butterflies in America. *Not for long,* I think. *I'm about to turn this place upside down, whether I'm ready to or not.*

We decide to relax for the rest of the afternoon since there is nothing pressing I need to do. I occasionally check my accounts, accepting friend requests along the way. It's getting bigger and bigger, and faster than I originally thought. More and more people are catching on, now that I uploaded pictures.

With that thought, I upload another picture to each account, linking them to one another again. The first gets the glass cube with space dust, while another gets the piece of metal. Even in picture form, you can tell it's unusual. I leave one small message with each, telling the nation that change is coming.

"That's all the pictures," I tell Brynn. "Hopefully, the message will really catch their interest."

"I'm sure it will. The pictures have already. Everyone will be chomping at the bit soon, trying to figure out what is going on."

"I know," I say. "Wherever we go from here, I'm pretty sure it's about to get crazy."

There's a knock at the front door, then the kids come barreling in. They fly over to us, and we get our hugs and kisses while we usher Brynn's parents back out the door. They try to make small talk, but we shut it down. With a final thanks, they are gone, leaving us once more without getting any new information from me.

As we begin dinner, the kids play. When it's time, they run in, scarf down their food, and run away again, eager to play as much as possible before bed. *I wish I had their energy,* I think to myself. *These days I'm tired by noon.*

We finally catch them, and fight to get them into pajamas and brush their teeth. Going to bed is like the end of the world to a toddler. Going without toys for eleven or more hours is the worst thing ever. After they watch their single episode of some crazy 'educational' cartoon, we walk them to their beds. Tucking them in, we tell them goodnight and decide to head to bed ourselves. *Each day seems to go by faster,* I think.

Lying in bed, my thoughts turn back to my last night on the Zavilisk again. I had lain there, in the same position, thinking the same thing I am now. *What am I getting myself into? This might be more than I can handle.* But my resolve wins again. I don't have a choice anymore. So I might as well do my best.

·· ● ··

We wake up the next morning to four extra bodies in the bed. The pokes, pulls and talking get us out of bed quick, and we start on their breakfast.

With the children fed, I get to work as they run around the house. My latest pictures and the accompanying message have been reposted and shared more than any others. *I guess it's time for the next step*, I realize.

I begin by opening up a picture editor. I create a collage, with most of the photos of the things I brought with me. On top of the pictures, I add the message: "The future is here. We need change to reach it."

Opening up my social media accounts, I type out a message for each.

"I need your help now, guys! Please post this picture anywhere you can. Every little bit helps! The future is here. What we do with it is up to us. We can't make it happen without major changes in the government. If we stand together as one, they can't knock us down. Don't let fear or complacency keep us from achieving greatness. Because that's what we're on the brink of. Greatness. Join me in the push for *REAL* progress."

I attach the collage I made, and post the messages.

"It's about to get real," I tell Brynn as she walks in the room. She sits beside me and reads what I've just posted.

"Wow," she says. "I've known it was coming, but I still can't believe it's that time already. Are you sure you're ready?"

"I don't really have a choice, now. Are you ready? I couldn't begin to tell you what happens now."

"I'm ready," she replies. "This has needed to

happen longer than we've been working on it."

She's right, I tell myself. I just never realized I'd be the one pushing for change.

I send a quick email to the scientists with a link to my posts, then open my bag. Reaching in, I pull out my radio again. Brynn eyes me, wondering what I'm doing, but doesn't ask.

"Kalis?" I ask.

A short wait, and then, "Hello, my friend! How is your progress?"

"It's going much faster than I thought. I'm going to need to reach other countries soon. How quickly can you get to the Milky Way?"

"We can be there in no time! This is great new, Ira. I was nor expecting things to move this quickly."

"I wasn't either," I tell him. "Apparently, the people here have been itching for something to latch on to. Now that it's here, they can't get enough. I've got them putting up posters now, trying to reach the people that were unreachable through the internet. My next step is to spread the message to the world."

"We are already working preparing the ship, my friend. We will be there shortly. I will let you know when we arrive."

"Sounds good, Kalis. I'll be waiting."

Almost immediately, Brynn says, "What in the world are you doing now?"

"Once they're in our galaxy, my internet traffic will be routed through their ship, bypassing the international firewall. Then I'll be able to get contact other countries and show them what I've shown everyone here."

"Wow. Every time I try, I can't imagine how advanced they really are. And now you tell me something like this, just adding to it. I'm truly amazed."

"I know," I say, placing the radio into my pocket. "Let's go see what those kids are up to while we wait."

Thirty minutes later, I hear the radio. "Ira?"

"Hey, Kalis," I respond.

"Good, good, I was hoping you would be near the radio," Kalis says.

"I've kept it with me since we talked. I wasn't expecting you to reach me again so quickly, though."

"Well, it does not take long for us to travel," he tells me. We are close enough for you to use our ship as a relay now. Your network has been reconfigured already. It is ready when you are."

"You don't waste any time, do you?" I ask.

"No, we do not, my friend. Especially not when something this big is happening."

"Well, I better get to it then."

"We will talk again soon, I'm sure. Take care, my friend."

"You too, Kalis," I say.

Putting the radio back in the bag, I grab my computer. I navigate to the most popular social media networks outside of the US and start the process all over again. Email, username and password, date of birth. Check, check, and check. I add popular people, and copy my original social media post over to the new websites, adding that I am living in the US, and am bypassing the firewalls just to get this message out.

"Another huge step," I tell Brynn, closing the computer.

"I know," she says. "What happens now?"

"We wait. I'll check on everything again tonight after the kids go to bed."

Nine hours later, I realize that I can't keep up with so many social networks receiving this much attention. Brynn and I break it up. She takes the US accounts, while I focus on those connected to the outside world.

I check my email before conferring with Brynn. I find emails from all three scientists, each supporting my decision to go public. They tell me they will be prepared to come to me whenever I'm ready.

Checking in with Brynn, I see that even more people have come on board. She continually shows me pictures. My signs are hanging everywhere. Telephone poles, bulletin boards, the front of buildings, all holding my sign, supporting my mission solely by existing. Others say that they've printed them off and are handing them out on street corners and supermarket parking lots.

And then, I see something that stops me in my tracks. A video, uploaded to a popular video sharing site, of a protest. The protesters have pickets, with my collage or other pictures I took stapled or glued to sticks they carry. They are chanting as well, with phrases like, "We want answers!" and, "Change for the future!" coming through my speakers. And they are being arrested. Every single one, being rounded up and handcuffed, stuffed inside police cruisers to face some unknown fate. *I don't even think there are enough jails to lock up every single one of these people.*

I feel terrible. All these people, high on hope, being arrested for something I started. I'm speechless, no words seem like the right thing to say. I picture the kids who have a parent that isn't going to be home tonight. Maybe longer. Something inside me breaks.

"It's not your fault," Brynn says. "These people have been oppressed for too long. They have been waiting for someone to lead them to they change they want. You just happen to be the person leading. What the government does right now is not up to you, though. That part is out of your hands. It is not your fault, Ira. This started when President Jacobs took office."

"I know. You're right." I tell Brynn. "But that doesn't change how bad I feel right now."

She kisses me, taking my hand in hers. "Let's watch a movie. Ignore this stuff for the rest of the night."

"Okay," I say. "Let's see what we can find on TV."

We settle in and find a movie, which turns out to be some five-year-old romance I've probably seen a million times. I don't care what it is. Right now, it doesn't matter. I just need to take my mind off of reality.

Reality, it seems, has different plans. At exactly eleven PM, our movie gets interrupted. A breaking news report flashes, hijacking my TV screen.

"We interrupt your regularly scheduled program to bring you this special news report. The office of the president has just released this statement:

'I just attended a briefing with my national security advisor. He has informed me of demonstrations across the country regarding one man having proof of alien life. I'm here to tell you that all of this is false, and these actions will cease. National curfews are being enacted. There will be no more protests. You are all well aware of the law. These illegal actions will be prosecuted to the greatest extent possible. And for the man who started this nonsense, I have a message. We will find you. The nation's best analysts are working on this twenty-four, seven. You can turn yourself in, or you can wait until we find you. But rest assured we will find you. You will be held accountable for your actions against this country.'

Again, that message was from President Jacobs. There will be a special segment in the morning for viewers to call and weigh in on these new developments. Please, though, remember the law when calling in. We cannot air any statements made against the president.

We apologize for any inconvenience. Please continue to enjoy your viewing experience."

Our movie comes back on, but neither of us are paying any attention. My mouth has been hanging open for two minutes straight. My skin is white with both rage and terror. Brynn's hand still covers her mouth, her eyes open wide.

"Brynn, honey," I say, my voice sounding as weak as I feel. "I think we need to go."

· 12 ·
Justice
The White House

"WHAT the hell does he think he's doing?!" President Jacobs shouts. He stares out the window of the oval office, studying the grass starting to grow on the White House lawn. "He can't just change the entire world. Its's preposterous!"

"I know sir. I agree," says the vice president.

"We need to figure out where he lives. Has anyone figured out his address yet?"

"They are working on it, sir. We're trying to utilize his local police department. Unfortunately, half of their officers are refusing to work, and the other half want nothing to do with taking down a man whom they respect. The University Police are even worse.

"Hell, Jim, we could drive there and search it today ourselves. It's not that damn far. Why are we using the locals?"

"Because it's their jurisdiction, sir. It's just the way these things work."

"Well work on changing it. I don't want to keep working through someone that isn't committed to helping us.

"Yes sir," the vice president says, walking over to stand at the window beside the president.

I can't believe this is happening, the president thinks. *I thought I had everything in place to ensure I never lost control.* "I will not give up control of my country," he says. "This is the most ridiculous thing I have ever heard. Aliens. What nonsense."

"Sir, I believe the general consensus is that it's all real."

"What?! Get someone in here. One of the analysts. Now! I don't believe it."

The vice president walks out, eager to get away from the president. He has his own opinion, and it is very different from that of the man he serves with.

I'd prefer to live in a world where no one has this much control. Even I didn't think he'd ever go this far. He finds an analyst and drags him back to the oval office.

Walking through the door, he sees the president pacing. His face is still red, his hands still clenched into fists. *I don't think I've ever seen him this mad before.*

"Tell me about this stuff Mr. Sanders supposedly has," the president says to the analyst, as soon as they walk through to door.

"Well, sir, we believe the items he has revealed so far are real."

"How could they be real?!"

"Sir, all we have is photographic evidence, so it's hard for us to be completely sure yet. But from what we can see, the metal has strange properties that we don't believe any other metal on Earth possesses."

"What about everything else?"

"Well, we certainly don't have any type of hologram technology that is anywhere near that level of sophistication. There's no way to be sure about the creature he posted pictures of, but I've never seen anything like it. We're consulting with paleontologists now to see if there is anything close in the fossil record."

"This is insane!" Jacobs shouts, his rage growing. "There is no way another civilization wants to help this worthless planet. There's not a damn thing here worth it."

"Well, what do you think they might want?" asks the vice president.

"Wait, don't tell me you believe this nonsense too!" he shouts again.

"Well, it's hard not to when the evidence is pointing that way."

"Jesus, Jim. It' fake. Elaborate, maybe, but fake all the same. But if I did have to guess, I'd say they wanted our resources. Water or oxygen or something."

"You really think someone that advanced would

come here just to steal our resources? Why not just go to a different planet and get them."

"We're probably ants to them," President Jacobs says. "They don't care if we're here or not. They just want to take what's ours. What we really need to do is prepare to defend ourselves."

"Defend ourselves?" the vice president asks.

"Yes! Defend ourselves, Jim! We need to be able to protect what we've got. We can't let some alien invasion happen on our soil."

"I honestly don't think that's what this is about, sir."

"Well, I don't care what you think, Jim. I want that damn technology."

"They're working as fast as they can, sir. As soon as they find something out, I'm sure they'll let us know."

"Even if they are peaceful, I don't see why in the world he would expect us to give up our country."

"Sir, I don't think he wants us to give it up. I think he just wants us to come together as one people. At that point, countries really don't matter anymore."

"I don't care what he wants either! I want to keep this nation strong. It got weak over the last two decades. Soft. I've just started making it strong again and now this?! There is no way I'm giving up everything I've worked so hard for."

"Not even if everyone else in the world has?"

"What the hell do you mean?"

"Sir, I can imagine the rest of the world is going to

welcome this change. If they do, we'll be the only ones fighting it. What do you think will happen then?"

"Well then I guess we'll be fighting the rest of the world and aliens," the president replies.

"Don't be ridiculous. They're not going to attack us. Our own people, however, might be another story."

"No one in the US has enough strength to stand up to me. You saw it during the election. It was a train wreck. I won because I was stronger."

"Sir," the vice president starts, "This is different. This is real change. This is the absence of power. And not because they don't want it, but because it would be unnecessary."

"Power is always necessary, just like war. None of it will end. This is just some crazy pipe dream of his, and he's made some damn props just to further his cause."

"I don't believe that's the case. I think you're just scared, sir. I think you don't like the idea of losing control because you won't have anything left."

"What the hell do you mean, I won't have anything left?! Don't you dare disrespect me, Jim."

"I don't mean any disrespect, sir. I'm talking about your legacy. The only things you have are the changes you've made. And the general public doesn't view them as good, anyways. Not making the changes the public is calling for would just push them away even further. So, you already walk a thin line. What good is a legacy if you're the only one that likes it, and everyone else hates you?"

"I don't care what the public thinks, Jim. I care about my country. They can think whatever they want. I'll still walk away after eight years knowing that I did what needed to be done. Knowing that I made a difference for the United States."

"Okay, sir," the vice president responds. *I couldn't disagree more.*

"I'll lay it out for you. I don't believe any of it. I want real evidence. I want the items he has, and I want them now. And I want him. I don't care how you have to get him. I want him brought to justice. If I have my way, which I damn well should, he'll see the death penalty for treason."

At this, the vice president snaps. "I want no part of it! I think you are acting ridiculous. I think you are a scared man who is abusing his power. I refuse to be associated with it any longer. You do what you want. I am done."

"You can't just quit. You're the Vice President of the United States! It doesn't work like that!"

"I'm well aware of how it works, Mr. President. I'm not quitting, I'm just not going to involve myself with sentencing a man to death for doing what he believes is right."

With that, he walks out the door. At the same time, a staffer runs in. "Mr. President, I think there's something you need to see."

"What now?"

"Sir, we've found a research grant you approved

for Mr. Sanders. It appears that he hasn't violated any laws. The local police have completely quit cooperating now."

"I authorized no such thing!" he screams now, his anger building up and flowing freely. "I would know if I authorized someone to research aliens! And he has violated plenty of laws, mainly treason for speaking out against me."

"Well sir, I just thought you should know, he's on a plane right now."

"Where is he headed?"

"It appears that his destination is Geneva, sir."

"He can't leave the country! It's not possible!"

"It is when he has authorization through his research grant. And sir, you didn't let me finish. There's more."

"What else could there be?"

"He has a layover right here at Ronald Reagan, before catching his next flight to Switzerland."

"Stop him, dammit! I don't care what it takes. He will be stopped. He is not allowed to leave this country. Ira Sanders will be brought to justice."

· 13 ·
The Chase
Charlottesville, Virginia

CHAOS. This is the only word to describe
what is happening in our house. Brynn
flies, throwing clothes into already stuffed suitcases,
grabbing food from the kitchen, and packing up any
toiletries she thinks's we'll need. I get my things from
the ship together, trying to be slow and methodical
instead of falling in line with Brynn's frantic rush to
leave. Focusing on what lies ahead, I begin formulating
a plan.

"What are we gonna do?" she asks, frantic.
"We have nowhere to go, Ira. We can't just live in
the car. How do you expect us to avoid the federal
government?"

"I have a plan, babe. Don't worry. We're gonna be fine." *I hope. What the hell am I getting us into?* "Just call your parents and get them to take the kids. I know it's late, but tell them it's urgent."

"You may have a plan, but I don't know it. I'm freaking out Ira. You're wanted!"

"I know, I know. Please just trust me. I'm gonna get us through this."

"Okay," she agrees, resigned. Unless she doesn't want to come with me, she doesn't really have a choice. And she knows it.

She makes the call, and we wake the kids. We get them ready to go and pack some clothes and pull-ups. We throw in a couple of their favorite toys and it seals the deal. Where the toys go, they follow. Brynn's parents are there within an hour, and they're not happy. I get the evil eye from them both before they go. I know I have a lot of explaining to do soon.

Once they go, Brynn and I load the car. She's still a mess, but calming down. She realizes that we need to be logical. And I understand that right now, it's hard for her to do so.

As an afterthought, I snap my computer open. I shoot out a quick message to the US social networks, telling them to keep up the push, and that I will not abandon this. I acknowledge the arrests that have been made and give my support to the arrestees and their families. I also send a quick email to the scientists, asking them to delete our emails and that I will do the same. I remind them of their vulnerability, since they've been communicating with me about all of this, and tell them that I will contact them when it is safe.

Stowing the laptop in my bag, I tell Brynn I'm ready. She hands me a to-go cup of coffee, and we zip out of the door. As we hop in the car, I turn it on and throw it in reverse while Brynn is still buckling in. We blast out of the driveway and down the hill, leaving the known behind and driving into the unknown ahead.

"So what's this great plan of yours?" Brynn asks.

"Well, I had Kalis gain access to the government's research databases," I tell her. "He added my name and a project to the list of people who have been granted permission to conduct research. He also transferred money to a bank account we set up for me, from the grant office that oversees research to fund our 'project.' The amount of money we have access to is a little staggering."

"Money is great," Brynn responds. "But how does that help us avoid capture?"

"Do you know what else comes with permission to conduct research? The ability to travel internationally."

"How did you think of all this?" Brynn asks. "And don't you think they'll be watching for you at airports?"

"I don't think so. My research proposal wasn't submitted through the formal channels. There is no real proposal. Kalis just entered their system and gave me the ability to do what I needed to do. So there's no reason for them to know that I have permission.

They shouldn't even know I can travel internationally. They probably don't even realize they're missing the money."

"Well, I hope you're right. I don't exactly want to get arrested for harboring a fugitive," Brynn says, giving me a smile.

"We're gonna be fine, Brynn," I say, reassuring myself as much as I am her. "Before we travel, though, I think we need to rest. They don't know who I am yet, so it should still be safe for us to get a hotel room. We'll leave in the morning to catch a plane."

"Okay. But I don't know if I'll be able to sleep."

"I don't know if I will either," I tell her. "But we have to try. We won't be thinking very clearly tomorrow with no sleep."

We keep driving, looking for a hotel that would suit our needs. After driving by three, we find one. A nondescript hole in the wall just outside of town, we decide it's perfect for laying low. We purchase a room with the money in the separate account, just in case they figure out my name by the morning. We take our bags in and crash into the bed, both exhausted.

I tell Brynn goodnight and turn out the bedside light before I begin the long process of running through the day in my head. I wonder if I'm doing the right thing, and if I've done my best in covering my tracks. I think about Brynn and if she's safe coming along with me. And I think about the future, and if I have even a remote possibility of making it happen.

··●··

The next morning, we wake up early. It's only been a few hours, but any sleep is better than no sleep. We pack our things in silence, both still too tired to strike up a conversation. We quickly load up the car again and abandon the room. Shooting for an early flight, we head straight for the airport across town. It's small, but it'll connect us to an international flight in DC.

On the way, I turn on the radio. "I wanna see if there have been any updates," I tell Brynn. I shift from station to station, trying to catch the news. Finally, I land on a station talking about the events of the past few days. They say they haven't heard anything more from the government yet. Unfortunately, that doesn't really mean anything to me. They could just be keeping the search quiet, hoping to catch me off guard.

Pulling into the airport, I take it slow. I circle the giant lot, making sure there are no extra police vehicles out. The last thing I need is to walk straight into their open arms. Satisfied no one is looking for me, we park. I choose the long term lot, since I'm unsure of how long we'll be gone. We grab a shuttle and ride to the terminal in silence.

Once we get there, I find a flight leaving for Reagan International and buy two one-way tickets. We should be in DC by 10 am. I load our suitcases onto the luggage conveyor, not wanting to carry anything but my bag onto the plane.

Now, the part I dread. We walk slowly, my nerves eating me up as we head toward the security checkpoint. We reach it, and I feel like my knees will give out at any time. Inching closer, it looks like all is normal. It doesn't appear that security has been heightened. We reach the bins, and I empty my pockets as I place my bag on the line. Brynn does the same. I take off my belt and shoes and place them inside as well. Walking forward, I step through the metal detector. No beep. *Thank God.* It turns out metal detectors can't even pick up whatever kind of special metal this stuff is made of. Brynn gets through fine as well and we gather our items without being stopped.

Walking towards our waiting area, Brynn asks, "How long do you think it'll be before they figure out that it's you they want?"

"I'm really not sure," I tell her. "It could be any time. I guess they could trace the IP address that the posts came from and figure it out. We'll see. Hopefully, we're in Great Britain before they figure it out."

We catch the news as we wait, and there are still no updates. *Good*, I think to myself. I just need a couple more hours.

A last minute idea pops into my brain, and I pull out my phone. I conduct a search, furiously typing and swiping. Finding what I'm looking for, I start to crank out an email.

"I need a place to stay. It won't be long. I hope you understand the urgency of this message. By the time you respond, I will be in the air, headed for an international airport. I will explain more when I get to you. If I had anyone else to ask, I would. You're the only person I know of that may be interested. Thank you."

I attach the pictures of the items from the ship. Next, I screenshot pictures from all of my social media posts and some of the reactions from across the US. Attaching these to the email as well, I click Send.

Our plane arrives at the gate, and we begin to board. Brynn seems surprised to see that our seats are first class. "I figured, why not?" I tell her. "Might as well when we've got the money. I've never flown first class before. Now seemed like a better time than ever."

Laughing, she says, "You're right. When we're paying with the government's money, why not splurge a little?"

"Exactly!" I say. "Enjoy it while we can."

The flight attendants begin their routine, and the Captain announces that our flight is about to take off. We taxi out to the runway, and I remember how impossibly slow it feels in such a fast aircraft.

Within minutes, we're wheels up. The flight levels off and everyone starts moving around. People find the restroom, and flight attendants pass out drinks. All Brynn and I can do is sit nervously and stare through the window, watching everything we know disappear behind us.

The flight doesn't take long, and before we know

it, we're descending. The Captain turns on the seatbelt sign while the flight attendants gather up the last few soda cans and cups. We level off again, and the Captain makes an announcement.

"I apologize folks, but there seems to be a delay. We'll be circling the airport while we wait for clearance to land. Please be patient, and I'll let you know when the situation changes."

I shoot a nervous glance at Brynn, who is already giving me the same look.

"That doesn't sound good," I tell her.

"I know," she responds, sounding even more nervous than she looks. "I hope it's not what my brain is telling me what it is."

"Me too," I say, turning to look back out the window.

The Captain comes back on the intercom and tells us that they've given him clearance, apologizing again for the wait. We begin descending again, and before long, the land outside is getting closer. We make the last turn, lining up with the runway, and begin our final descent. I feel the wheels bump the ground a minute later, and we begin the rapid deceleration. We reach taxi speed, and start the slow drive toward our gate.

That's when I see them. It seems impossible. So many flashing lights, all in one spot. We don't head to the gate. We head straight for the lights.

"Ira..." Brynn starts. "I think they've figured out who you are."

"I think so," I say, worry washing over me.

Staring out the window again, I can see now that most are police. However, there are a few news vans as well, invited by the government to document the capture of a wanted man. This gives me an idea.

Grabbing my bag from above my seat, I pull out the radio Kalis gave me.

"Kalis!" I say, hoping to get his attention quickly. We don't have much time. The plane is almost to the line of police cars already.

"Hello, my fri-," he gets out before I cut him off.

"Kalis, I need your help, quick. Your ship. Can it move me to a different location, the same way it brought me to you?"

"Yes, this is possible," he says. "How soon do you need us to move you, and where?"

"Patch into Channel 13 News in Washington DC and keep an eye on their live video. You'll see me soon. Once Brynn and I are on the ground, move us. I can't tell you the location out loud. Check my email. You'll see the last one I sent. Send us to the recipient's house. Can you handle that?"

"Not a problem, my friend. We are ready. I see that your government isn't very receptive to what you've been doing."

No, they're not," I tell him. "But it doesn't matter. The public will push them to do what is right. They can't hold out forever. I just need to be out of their reach until they calm down."

"I understand. We will get you where you need

to go."

"Thank you, Kalis," I say sincerely. "We'll talk again soon." Putting the radio back in my bag, I notice the weird looks I'm getting from the passengers around me. I ignore them. Now is not the time for explanations.

Turning to Brynn, I warn her. "You're not going to like what is about to happen. They're going to arrest me, and surely you too. But we won't be going with them. You're about to feel what I felt when they brought me onto their ship. Trust me?"

"You're right. I don't like it. But yes, I trust you. I'm ready."

Just in time, in fact. The plane stops, and we hear the megaphone after the engines cut off. "Ira and Brynn Sanders, you are both under arrest. When the door opens, exit the plane with your hands above your head."

We hear the door being unsealed, and then it swings open. "Well, here goes nothing," I tell Brynn as I slide my bag over my shoulders. "I love you, babe."

"I love you too," she says as we walk towards to door.

As I turn the corner, I raise my hands. I won't be needing them anyway. We descend the steps slowly, and my eyes scan the crowd before us. I see the news crew, directly behind the police officers waiting for us.

"Interlace your fingers behind your head," they tell us.

We do as we're told as we reach the bottom. They

tell us to stop as they walk towards us. And then it happens.

The great ball of electricity appears beside us. The crowd goes silent. Even the police officers stop. But without a doubt, the cameras continue rolling.

"My God," Brynn says, her eyes wide with awe. "It's amazing."

"Get ready babe. You're about to experience something that only two humans before you ever have. And it might feel a little weird."

"I'm as ready as I'm gonna get," she replies.

The ball continues growing, its brightness rivaling the natural light now. It's an odd sensation, being outside and seeing something that outshines the daylight. It has broken the limit for most people now, as everyone has averted their eyes.

And then, finally, it starts. The growing static reaches out and touches us, seemingly warning us of what is about to happen. Brynn's grip on my hand tightens, but I don't even feel it.

The world goes black as electricity fills our bodies.

·14·
The Call
Geneva, Switzerland

Y eyes open immediately, and I remember where I should be. *I'm getting better at this.* Brynn, this having been her first time, didn't fare so well. She's still lying beside me, eyes closed. I sit up and look around. The house seems surprisingly average. Definitely European, and old. But nice, in a normal kind of way.

"Where are we?" Brynn asks, waking up.

"We're currently inside the Director of CERN's house. I emailed him right before we got on the plane, hoping he'd take us in. I guess we're about to find out," I say as I hear footsteps coming down the hallway in front of us.

"My goodness, when you asked if I would allow you to stay here, I had no idea you'd just show up inside my home three hours later," he says, in a thick Swiss accent. "But here you are, nonetheless. When you check your email, you will see that I agreed to allow you to stay here. I don't suppose it matters now, though. Here you are!"

"Yeah, sorry for dropping in on you like this," I tell him. "I wasn't planning on it to happen like this. Thank you, though. I'm Ira Sanders, and this is my wife, Brynn."

"It's nice to meet you, Ira. You as well, Brynn. I'm Simon, as you know, the Director of CERN. I must say, I was rather intrigued after reading your email. How am I to believe that this is not just an elaborate hoax on your part?" He walks us down the hallway, and we find ourselves in a living room. Brynn and I take a seat on a couch while Simon sits in an armchair.

"How about I show you?" I ask, pulling my bag in front of me. I pull out the bar for the holographic screen and set it up. Turning it on, I pass my hand in front to start up the video feed. It appears, and I'm surprised to see that it is a video feed of the cockpit area of the Zavilisk. I can see everything from the Navigation area to the large windows in front. It looks as if Alter is there.

Pulling out my radio, I say "Alter?"

Without pause, the pilot chair spins, and Alter steps down. "Ira? Hello! I assume you are accessing the video feed?"

"I am," I tell him. "Can you step closer? I need my wife and associate to see you better."

"Of course, course! It is good to hear from you, Ira. I hope you are making some progress?"

"I'm getting there. It's going faster than I thought, honestly. However, I am also currently on the run from my government."

"I am sorry to hear that, but I'm sure all will be better soon," he says, stepping up to the camera.

"How interesting," Simon says. "His skin is such an interesting color. Almost… translucent. And I can see details, like his ears and eyes, which make it quite obvious he is not of this planet."

"Ira, I thought you'd like to know, the news station you directed us to was recording live. So everyone, including the president, saw what happened. I assume this will further your cause."

"I'm sure it will. Thank you, Alter. We'll talk again soon."

"Take care, Ira. You as well, Brynn."

"Believe me now?" I ask Simon.

"In fact, I do. Thank you for sharing such a wonderful discovery with me. How do you fit in, though? What can I do to help?"

As I pack the holographic screen away, I begin describing what the past week has been like for me. I tell him about everything I went through and everything I learned on the ship. Then, I explain to him what it has been like since I've been home. Finally, I tell him how I fit into all of this.

"They were going to invite Earth to join the community," I say. "They were just a few years away. But then our new president screwed it up. They asked me to fix it. We came up with a plan, and here I am. You weren't part of it originally, but I sure am glad you are now."

"Well, I'm happy to help. What other gadgets might you have in that bag?

I pull out the square of metal and cylinder with the bug inside. Removing it from the canister, I place it on the table in front of me. Finally, I remove the glass cube containing the dust. I know this will be his favorite, so I hold on to it while he studies everything else.

"This metal is nothing like I've ever seen before," he says, admiring the spread before him. "And what is this creature?"

"That is an alternative life form. It is silicone based, rather than carbon-based as we are. They tell me that most of them are like this. They are not dangerous, other than blocking vision when they swarm together. They mostly live on planets with no atmosphere, which would explain why we've never seen them here on Earth. Apparently, our planet isn't conducive to prolonging their life, either."

"It's quite an interesting specimen," he tells me.

"This is what I think you really want to see," I say, handing him the cube.

"What is it?" he asks.

"Inside of that cube is a bit of dust from the center

of the universe. It is the oldest material ever held by mankind. And you can see as well, it actually has a glow to it."

"It's amazing," he says. "But I still don't understand. What do we need to do to join this community?"

"We need to end famine, pollution, and war," I tell him flatly.

"Well isn't that an undertaking."

"It's actually coming along quite well. The US is already in disarray. And I've posted messages on the most popular social networks outside of the US as well. I haven't had a chance to check on those, but I'm sure they're getting plenty of attention by now. I just need to get the president to open his eyes and we'll be good I think."

"I think he'd be crazy to ignore what he and everyone else saw before you got here," Brynn says.

"Me too, but we'll have to wait and see."

With that, I pull my laptop out of my bag. I open up the non-US social networks and check on my progress as we talk. Europe and Asia are already on board, and they haven't even seen any pictures yet. I post all of them this time, along with the screenshots I took earlier.

Finished with that, I pull out the radio again and call for Kalis. He answers quickly.

"Ira, my friend! I am so glad you made it to your destination. That was good thinking, asking us to help. What can I do for you now?"

"Can you transfer television signals here from the US?"

"Of course, I can! Give me just a second."

I picture him standing in front of a screen like the one we used a bit ago with a keyboard in his lap, typing commands the same way we do. However, this is probably the farthest thing from what he is actually doing. *I doubt hacking is all code to them,* I think.

As soon as I finish the thought, he's done. "Okay, Ira. Your television will now cycle through American channels when you press the channel button on the remote. If you wish to switch back to Swiss television, just press the source button."

"Thanks a lot, Kalis," I tell him

We turn on the TV, and sure enough, the first channel to appear is an American major news network. And even that channel, controlled by the government, is showing what happened at the airport.

They then cycle through feeds from around the country, all showing the same thing. Riots. Everywhere. New York, Los Angeles, Dallas, every major city is in dishevel. People have even begun looting, and the police are powerless.

"It's starting," I say, surprised to see how crazy everything has gotten.

"I'd say it has. They aren't messing around, are they?"

"No, they really aren't. The president won't be able to hold out much longer. The people will be beating down the White House door soon if he doesn't do the right thing. No one will stand for anything less after seeing so much evidence."

"It appears your plan is working after all," Simon interjects. "Thankfully, I don't think you'll have much trouble anywhere else in the world. We are an open-minded bunch."

"Thank goodness for that," I respond. "I'd hate to see the rest of the world reacting like this."

"So would I," he replies with a laugh.

I decide now to post one more message on my American social media accounts. Pulling them up, I begin.

"Thank you all so much for continuing to push for what is right. Keep it up! I will be right there with you again soon. I told you all I wouldn't abandon you, and I haven't. Do not allow yourselves to be oppressed anymore. Stand up to this administration, and for the future. The rest of the world now knows everything you know. And they know what is going on in the US. It won't be much longer, friends. The president can't hold out forever.

And by the way, President Jacobs. If you're still looking for me, you can stop. I'm in Geneva, so good luck. When you wanna talk, call me. I sure hope your analysts have figured out my number by now."

With that, I snap a picture of Brynn and me with Simon, attach it to the post, and hit Enter.

"If that doesn't seal the deal, I don't know what

will," I say to no one in particular.

We continue talking as we flip through the channels, all showing the same thing, just with a different channel logo.

"I didn't think about this at the time I sent the email," I begin, "You were just the first person I thought of that might wish to assist me. But you are an important figure in Europe, especially among the science community. Could you set up some meetings with me? Do you have that kind of pull?"

"Well, I think I could work something out," Simon responds. "It depends on who you need to speak with."

"How about the leaders of Switzerland and France, to start?"

"Oh, I can definitely make that happen. And if it goes well, I'm sure they will push other countries to meet with you as well."

"That's perfect," I say. "I want to wait, though. I'm holding out hope that the president will contact me. If I can get him to come around, I have no doubt the rest of the world will follow suit. If the US can get on board with something like this, then everyone will."

"I agree. With your country the way it is right now, the world will flip when your president changes his ways. Let me go make some calls. I should, at least, let them know that you are requesting a meeting. It will give them time to prepare. I'll start some dinner for us as well."

"Thanks," I reply. "Please, just don't tell them anything else that I've told you. I need to keep that information guarded until I can tell them myself."

"Of course, I understand that. I will only tell them what is happening in the US and advise them to look at our social media websites. That alone should give you their attention."

With that, he sets off. Brynn and I continue talking about my next step. We also discuss the need for new clothes and toiletries, since our suitcases are probably in federal custody right now. We can hear Simon in the other room, pots and pans clinking as he talks, his voice at times becoming animated. We decide it's going well though it's hard to tell when he is speaking in French. Thankfully, most of the elite throughout Europe speak English as well, so my eventual meetings should not require a translator.

Soon he has returned, inviting us to eat. As we sit down, he tells us how his phone calls went.

"Both the French and Swiss are very interested," he says. The Swiss Council has been following your posts on social media already, but they were still surprised to hear how much things have deteriorated in the US. France, on the other hand, had not seen any of your posts. I explained to the president and prime minister what is going on, and they agreed to meet you here when you meet the Swiss Council."

"Great!" I tell him. "Thank you so much. There are three American scientists I have spoken with as well, and I promised them that I would allow them to be the first to study the materials I have brought with me. I don't think they'll mind if I invite you to join them. I'm sure your expertise will be needed eventually anyway."

"I would love that," Simon responds. "I appreciate the opportunity to play a role in something as important as this. Thank you, Ira."

We continue eating, and Brynn and I enjoy the authentic Swiss meal he has prepared for us. We talk about what we hope will happen soon, and how important it is for the world.

"How exactly did you get here, anyway?" Simon asks randomly.

"Well, I can't really say," I begin. "Not because I can't or won't tell you, but because I do not know. It's one of the few things my hosts aboard the Zavilisk wouldn't tell me. There are things that they cannot tell us until we decide we are ready to join the universal community."

"Aah, this is understandable. The last thing they must want is for us to use their technology in ways that are against their values, or even worse, use it against them."

"Yes, exactly," I agree, thinking back to what my hosts told me aboard the Zavilisk. *I won't let it happen, this time. I'm hand picking the scientists. I will not allow anyone to take control of this process from me.* "That would be terrible."

After dinner, we move back into the living room. I check in on the social networks as we watch the TV.

We didn't think it could get any worse in the US, but it has. The police aren't even visible now. Some may even have joined in by now. The government still hasn't released a new statement, though. Judging by what's happening, that may actually be a good thing. If there is no statement, it could mean that they are finally considering an alternative to denying everything.

The social networks, both in the US and the rest of the world, have exploded again. After my new series of posts, they've been shared thousands of times. Everyone in the world is asking for the change I seek, and I can't see anyone still arguing that this is all false. Finally, it seems, the world is moving in the right direction.

Simon asks us what we think the world will be like if we do join the universal community. In the middle of discussing this, my phone rings. The sound is so unexpected, it startles all three of us. Checking the caller ID, the screen says 'Private.' I answer the call and turn on speakerphone, and my heart hits my throat while Brynn and Simons' eyes grow wider than I thought possible.

What we hear is, "Please hold for the President of the United States."

·15·
Bending Rules
Geneva, Switzerland

I STARE at Brynn, stunned. Speechless. It's a good thing the president isn't on the line yet, because I wouldn't have been able to get any words out yet anyway. After what seems like forever, an idea forms in my brain, spurring me into action.

"Brynn, grab your phone and turn on the voice recorder. We need to record this call."

Brynn jerks into action, frantically digging her phone from her pocket. Just as she gets the voice recorder app turned on, we hear the line pick up.

"Mr. Sanders, so nice of you to answer," I hear, the unmistakable voice of President Jacobs on the other end.

"I wasn't actually expecting you to call," I say. "Will you be paying the charge for this international call?"

"Anyway," he says, ignoring me. "I'm willing to drop the treason charges I originally had filed. I want you to come in and talk to me. Personally."

"And why would that be, Mr. President?"

"Well, to be blunt, the last thing we want is for any other countries to end up with the technology you have in your possession. It seems like what you have could set us years ahead of the rest of the world."

I end the call.

"What the hell?!" yells Brynn. "Why did you just hang up on him?!"

"Because, he needs to understand that he is not in control of this situation. And I will absolutely not hand over what I have just so he can try to weaponize it. It's never gonna happen."

"But this is just gonna piss him off more!" Brynn shouts, still upset.

"I don't care. Let him be angry. We're here, and he's there. There is nothing he can do. I will not allow him to use this to appease the public while the whole time, he's just doing it for his own benefit. No. He'll call back anyway. Don't worry."

Sure enough, a minute later, he did. And this time, there was no hold message. The call came directly from him, and not an operator.

"Sorry, Mr. President. We seemed to have lost the connection there. What is it you were saying?"

"I was saying, Mr. Jacobs, that I do not want you to give those items to any other country."

"Stop," I say. "Don't say it again unless you want the call to drop."

"How dare you-"

"No, how dare you," I say, cutting him off. "What makes you think you can call me and make demands when I am not even in the country? How do you think the public will react when I upload this recording to my social media accounts? I'm going to change the world, Mr. President. And if you don't want to change with it, I'm sure they will be willing to do it for you."

"Are you threatening me?!"

"No, sir. It's a promise."

"I'm going to make a call to Interpol," he threatens.

"No, you won't," I say. "Because then, they'll take what I have into evidence, and I can assure you it would eventually make it into hands even worse than yours. You know that."

"The United States WILL get that technology," he tells me. "I will use whatever means necessary."

"That may be so. But not before the rest of the world does. So there is still no benefit to you. There is no way for you to win here, Mr. President. Just accept that and we can move on. There are much more important things at stake."

"Like what?!" he yells. "What could be more important than national security?!"

"Like the fact that this would end the need for national security altogether."

"What in the hell are you talking about? There will always be a need for it."

"Not if I get my way, Mr. President."

"What could possibly eliminate the need for national security?" he asks.

"That's a conversation for us to have in person."

"Okay, let's talk hypothetically here," he says, after a pause. "If we were to have this conversation in person, would you bring the items you have with you back to the states?"

"Of course, I would."

"Okay. Then I will agree to meet you. You can come to my office. Call me when you get back to the states. You will not be arrested or hassled in any way," he says, giving me his number.

"No," I say as I write it down. "It will be in public, at a location of my choosing. You can bring your secret service. That is fine. But I will not do this in your office."

"Fine. Where?"

"I'll tell you when I get there," I tell him. "I have your word I will not be messed with in any way?"

"You have my word."

"Okay then. I will see you tomorrow. Goodbye, Mr. President," I say, hanging up the phone.

Ending her recording, Brynn looks at me. "Wow. I had no idea you'd stand your ground the way you did."

"It wasn't that bad. I was confident because I was right. There was no way he was going to win that argument. Not when I'm currently the only authority on the subject."

"Can you really trust him, though?" Simon asks.

"Not as far as I can throw him. But I don't need to yet."

"What do you mean?" Brynn asks. "You told him you'd bring the stuff with you. What makes you think he wouldn't just take it and have you arrested anyway?"

"Oh, I know he would. That's why I won't be taking it there with me. I didn't agree to take it to the meeting. I agreed to bring it back to the states. And we have a recording of that if we really need to prove it to anyone. It doesn't matter right now, though. I need to call Kalis, and I think we'll be in the clear."

"Why?"

"Because I need to get the rules bent a little," I say, pulling out the radio. "Kalis?"

"Hello, my friend! How is it going there on Earth?"

"I just spoke with President Jacobs on the phone," I begin. "I need a favor."

"Anything," he offers. "I will do whatever I can."

"Well, I'm not so sure this time. I need to get a rule bent a little bit. I am going to meet the president. But I will not be taking my things from the ship with me. The only other people I know who can keep them safe are the four scientists I have been in contact with. One, you already know as the owner of the house I am in.

"What are the chances we can allow them to study the items while I am with the president? I do not want him to have access to them whatsoever until the rest of the world has made the decision to join the universal community. I sincerely trust these scientists to do the right thing and follow any restrictions we set in place. I just believe that after I have talked with the president, and after they make a public announcement that the items are authentic and not of this world, President Jacobs will have absolutely no choice but to go along with my plan."

"You make a compelling argument," Kalis says. "Let me speak with the Captain and Birkim. I will get back to you shortly."

"Thank you, Kalis," I say, putting the radio down. Turning back to Brynn and Simon, I say, "Well, now I guess we wait."

While we wait, we make small talk. No one wants to get too excited in case this part of the plan falls through. Fortunately, it doesn't take Kalis long at all to get back to me.

"Ira?" he begins.

"I'm here, Kalis."

"To be brief, you will be allowed to take this step out of order. We spoke with the council, and they agreed that the extreme nature of the situation allows for a bit of leeway. But be careful. If you lose trust in one of the scientists at any time, please remove the items from their care immediately."

"I will, Kalis," I say, a grin spreading across my

face. "You have my word. Thank you so much."

"You are very welcome, my friend. It is the faith that we have in you that allows us to agree to this change. You should be thanking yourself."

"I'll talk to you soon," I tell him.

"I look forward to it," he replies.

Looking back up to Brynn and Simon, my grin breaks into a smile. "Who wants to go catch a plane?"

"We won't be needing to do that," Simon says.

"What do you mean?" I ask, puzzled.

"CERN has a private jet, Ira. We'll take that."

··●··

Landing in DC around 8 am, I actually feel refreshed. First class in the commercial jet was nice, but it was nothing compared to the luxury of a private jet. We flew throughout the night, and I slept the entire trip.

The night before, after talking with the president, I sent a quick email to the three US scientists. I told them when and where to meet us, and that I was adding Simon to their party because of all of the help he has provided, and his expertise in the field of particle physics. After that, we immediately packed and left.

Now, we are on our way to meet them. The first stop, though, was to get Brynn and I a rental car. I'm going to need her with me today.

"Are you nervous?" asks Brynn.

"I am," I tell her. "This could still go horribly wrong. While I know he won't get his hands on the technology, he could still have me arrested. It won't benefit him, but he seems spiteful like that."

Pulling into the now shuttered NASA office in DC, the three scientists are already waiting for us. After the president had shut everything down, he didn't completely end the space program. He just handed it over to the Air Force and closed all NASA offices. Today, it doesn't matter. This building makes the perfect place for the scientists to gather and study.

Getting out of the car, we have a quick meet and greet. We then make our way to the locked doors. Fortunately, the locks were never changed, and the ex-Director never notified anyone that he had a spare key. We walk right through the front doors, with no one outside noticing anything wrong.

I drop my bag and remove the radio. "I have to keep this on me," I tell them. "Everything else stays here for you to study. Run what tests you can before I get back. The first thing you need to focus on is proving that none of the metal can be found on Earth. After that, shoot for validating that the technology is outside of the production capabilities of any Earthly company. Text me when you are done, so that I can tell President Jacobs. I may call you afterward."

"No problem," says Simon. "We will be ready."

"Good luck, gentleman," I tell them. "And enjoy. It's not every day someone gets an opportunity like this. I will see you all soon."

Brynn and I turn and leave, directing our rental to the spy store downtown.

Here, we pick up a few things Brynn will need. We get a directional microphone that looks like a camera, for Brynn to direct at us. This way, she can record my conversation with the president from afar, without looking suspicious. We also get a button camera for me. It's small enough to not be noticed, but has excellent video quality.

Reaching the rental again, we continue past it. I call the president as soon as we walk.

He picks up on the third ring. "Hello, Mr. Sanders."

"Hello, Mr. President. You can meet me in the exercise section of Seaton Section Park at 10 am. It's small. You'll know it when you see it. Call me when you get there."

"I will see you then," he says, hanging up the phone.

Brynn and I keep walking as I explain to her my plan. I want to keep the president thrown off as much as possible. She agrees just as we reach our destination.

"I love you, Brynn," I tell her.

"I love you too," she says, her voice filled with worry.

"This will work. Trust me." With one final squeeze of my hand, she walks away, taking up her position while I head towards mine.

A few minutes later, my phone rings. *Here we go.*

"I'm here, Mr. Sanders. Where are you?"

"Change of plans," I tell him. "Head into the National Air and Space Museum. I'll be inside the Einstein Planetarium."

"That's not what we agreed on," he says. "Why the location change?"

"I didn't want your secret service men to get there before me," I tell him, giving him the truth. "I don't exactly trust you."

"Understandable," he replies, "But unfortunate. I'm canceling."

"Then you lose your last chance to talk to me or see anything. It'll be gone forever along with me. Take care, Mr. President."

"Wait, dammit. Just wait," the president says, pausing. "Fine, I'll be there soon."

I hang up the phone and try to wipe away my nervousness. It's not going to happen. I don't think anything will go wrong, but it's hard to say. And I'm not excited to be meeting a man I've grown to hate.

Just as I expected, the room suddenly clears out and the lights come on. *Subtle.* But it doesn't matter. Brynn is sitting on a bench outside the room, her back against a fighter jet. She's reading a magazine, the directional microphone that looks like a camera hanging from her neck, pointed directly at the opening to the planetarium.

The secret service clears the room, leaving me in place, and in walks the President of the United States.

"Hello, Mr. Sanders. It's about time we met."

·16·
Threats
Washington, DC

I LOOK to my right, still processing what is happening. *I'm meeting the president.* "Hello, Mr. President," I say.

He sits beside me, looking much more tired than I remembered. And grey.

"So what is it again that you wanted to talk to me about?" he asks. "Aah, that's right. You wanted to tell me how to eliminate the need for national security."

"You really need to stop looking at it that way, Mr. President. It's not about national security anymore. We're not going to take over the world with what I have, if that's what you think."

"Before we get into that," he starts, "Why don't you show me the items you brought."

"I didn't bring them with me."

His face turns red, enraged. I can see his anger building before my eyes.

"That is the only reason you came, isn't it?" I sneer, angry now.

"You're damn right it is! Now where the hell is it?"

"Safe," I tell him. "Somewhere you'll never find it. Because you don't need to. That's not what this is about."

"Dammit Ira, don't play games with me. I told you on the phone, we will have that technology. Do I have to have these men take you into custody to do it?"

"Touch me, and the technology is gone for good. And along with it, every opportunity to make the world a better place. I mean that. Look at my face. I know you can see just how serious I am. I do not play games, Mr. President. None of this has been a game. It has all been to prepare the US for what is needed.

"And what is that?" he asks. "What's needed? Tell me what you think is going on."

"I know what is going on. I'm more confident on that than I have been of anything else in my life. The technology really is from an alien species, Mr. President."

"Yes, my analysts eventually brought me to the same conclusion. I know that already."

"Well, Mr. President, let me explain to you why I have the items then. I brought them with me just to show them to the world."

"Why? Most of the world already believe that aliens exist. And why would another species allow you to leave with their technology just to show it off?"

"Because, sir, they have an agenda as well."

"And what might that be?"

"To enable us to have that technology as well," I tell him. His eyes widen a bit.

"Then why the hell are you keeping it from me?!"

"Because it's not just about you! It's not about turning it into weapons! It's about making the world a better place. And there is so much more to it than just getting our hands on a few bits of technology."

"Like what?"

"The universe is teeming with life, Mr. President. Absolutely full of it. There are thousands, millions of other intelligent species."

"So what? I don't care about that right now. If anything, it's all the more reason for us to study and exploit these things you have. We'll need to have the ability to defend ourselves."

"No, we won't."

"And why not, Mr. Sanders?"

"Because they're not violent."

"None of them? Bull."

"I'm serious. None. Not a single species that is capable of traveling throughout the universe has any intention of harming anyone else. They are peaceful. All of them."

"How do you know all of this anyways?"

"They told me, Mr. President. They brought me

aboard their ship and taught me everything."

"Why? What are you here for now?"

"To tell you, Mr. President, if you'd let me. And to tell the world."

"To tell us what?" he asks. "What could they have possibly wanted us to know?"

"To tell you that we have the opportunity to join them."

His eyes grow wide for a second. I can see him thinking, trying to come up with a retort. He's too defensive. He can't seem to get out of the mindset that everyone is out to get him.

Finally, he speaks again, though with a much different message than what I had hoped for. "I don't care. I want that technology. To hell with the rest of the world and space. The United States can become the world power it once was. I intend to make it that way."

I jump from my seat and vault two rows of seating in front of me, getting clear of the agents blocking the aisle. Walking between the seats to the main aisle in front of me, I say, "I think I'll catch a ride back to Europe. Good luck, Mr. President. There is absolutely no way you get your hands on any of it. It'll be gone before I am."

"Now, wait. Just wait. Hold on a minute," he says, stalling. "Just give me a minute to think." As he says this, I can see his secret service agents inching closer.

"No. I will not. The opportunity is now gone. Goodbye, Mr. President."

"Wait!" he shouts, frustrated. *Good,* I think to myself. I need him off of his game.

"Mr. President, there is so much more that I have not explained to you yet. But you don't care to hear it. All you can think about is yourself. I'm done with it. I'll let the rest of the world decide. You don't need to be involved at that point."

"Well tell me, dammit. Just tell me. I'll listen." He doesn't like the idea of not being involved with something everyone else in the world is involved in.

"Let me ask your agents first. I'd like to hear their opinion." I spin, looking them all in the eyes. There seem to be more of them.

"Would you guys want to hear more? Are you interested in this at all? Interested in how it can affect every single one of you? Interested in how it can make the world a better place?"

I get the occasional small nod, but no verbal responses. *If anything, they're professional.*

Heading back to my seat, I try to figure out where to begin. I decide on the beginning. I'll walk him through all of it if he'll let me, only omitting things that he doesn't need to know yet.

"Okay. Will you listen now?" I ask.

"I'm all ears."

"Billions of years ago, one alien species found another. They were very advanced, and taught the new species everything they knew. They then decided to search for other species and teach them as well. They eventually developed a council and came up with rules. Each species had to meet a certain standard before they were shown new possibilities. As you can imagine, the number of advanced life forms has now grown exponentially.

"They don't war. They don't hate. All they do is help each other. The council furthers this by seeking out other species in hopes of helping them too. They have research ships that they send out. These ships monitor species that they think are close to being ready. They call them brink species. When it's time, they make contact and begin the process."

"So that's what you are? The initial contact? They start the process here now?"

"Not exactly. I am not the initial contact. When they decide it's time, they land on the planet they are researching. They find and speak with world leaders, and form a council on the planet as well. This council, consisting of world leaders and scientists and such, then decide if their species is ready to take the next step."

"Then what are you?" the president asks. "What purpose do you serve?"

"I'm here as a liaison, basically. An intermediary."

"But, why?"

"Because, Mr. President, they were only a few years from making contact with Earth. That is, until you took office and made changes that set the entire planet back by decades."

"How dare you -"

"Not this again. No, how dare you. Look past

your anger for a minute. It's the truth. Look at what we could be doing, instead of closing ourselves off to the rest of the world. Look at the damage you caused. I don't care about your hurt feelings, Mr. President. I care about this planet and our species. I care about where we could be going."

"I have no control over that."

"You don't now, no. The rest of the world can fix this for us. You do not need to be involved."

"What do you mean, 'fix this?' What is the rest of the world going to do?"

"Mr. President, they decided to use me as a liaison because they think there is still hope for us. They are hoping that I can advocate for the change that needs to happen. And if I can, they want to do for us what they have for so many other species. They want us to join them in the universe."

"Well, what do we need to do? What needs to change?"

"You're not going to like it," I begin. "First, the walls need to come down. We need to stop sealing ourselves off from the rest of the world. This means through immigration as well as the transfer of information, so the firewalls need to go as well.

"Also, funding needs to be reallocated to research. And the stipulation that it all has to go through you should stop as well. Research and education have always been extremely important to us and the rest of the world. How can we possibly hope to be as smart as the rest of the universe if we can't even conduct research that doesn't involve defense?

"We need to do our part to end pollution as well. The Earth will not last much longer if we continue to destroy it. Ending famine is another step. No one should be allowed to die of starvation on a planet so full of things that nurture us.

"You cannot continue to prosecute those who question your actions, either. Questioning our leaders is part of what makes us a Democracy. If we can't weigh in on what is going on, then we aren't coming together as one.

"This is what it all comes down to, Mr. President. Coming together as one. The last thing on the list is ending war. There is no need to fight over resources when they are so abundantly available throughout the universe. So war is unnecessary. We will be one species. Race doesn't matter. What continent we're from doesn't matter. We are essentially one big family. Would you go to war against your brother? In the big picture, Mr. President, war is unnecessary on Earth, when everyone else in the entire universe is peaceful."

"There is no way," he huffs. "We can't end pollution or war. It's not possible."

"It's not impossible when every other country in the world is pushing for the same thing," I tell him. "Other countries are rioting and protesting as well. Everyone else in the world wants the same thing the people here in the US to do. They want to move forward, instead of staying the same or moving backward. We're stalled right now, Mr. President.

Stagnant. We need to change that."

"I still don't see it. There are countries that want nothing more than to go to war with someone."

"They can't do that without an Army," I say. "And they won't have an Army when everyone only wants world peace, so that we may attain the level of advancement that everyone else in the universe has achieved."

"I just don't know."

"I think the only choice you can make now is the right one. It's entirely too easy. Everyone wants you to take a step forward. I made sure of that before our meeting began."

"What do you mean?"

"The entire time I've been back on Earth, I've done nothing but prepare, sir. The messages on social media, the trip to Europe, everything. It was all in preparation for this moment. There are other things I've done that you aren't even aware of yet. You can't say no when the world is ready to explode.

"Quit stalling. Quit thinking about yourself. Think about the rest of the world, Mr. President. Yes, you will continue to look bad in some people's eyes. But so what? To others, you will be the man who saw the error in his ways, and was humble enough to fix it. That says a lot about someone's character. Be that man. Imagine where humans will be in ten years. In twenty. Clear across the universe, mining for iron or silicon to bring back here. There won't even be a need for currency."

"That is what I think about," he says. "There won't be a need for world leaders, either."

"All things considered, that's would be a step forward from where we are now," I spit, getting irritated. "That means we're a smart, peaceful society that doesn't need someone to hold our hand and tell us the right thing to do. But, there will always be a need for some type of leadership. Someone to decide which planet to mine, or what new technology to develop. Don't allow these worries to keep you from seeing the big picture. If we want our planet and people to survive, we need to do this."

"I'm not going to push for something I don't think is possible."

"Well, it comes down to this," I begin. "You can save what little is left of your reputation and push for the rest of the world to accept this great change, while at the same time putting the US back to the way it was. Or, you can continue to always be known as the man who wanted to halt progress. For the entirety of our life as a species, everyone will know your name. They will know that you are the man that tried to stop the people of Earth from advancing, and was overrun by the very people he was trying to repress. The choice is entirely up to you, for now. But rest assured, the world will make their decision, whether you're involved or not. And if you're not involved, it won't be good for you. Because I can guarantee you, these walls will come down. Things will change. You just might not be around to see it happen."

"Was that a threat?"

"No, sir. That was me telling you what would happen. I wouldn't personally do anything, or ever advocate violence. But I can guarantee that when the entire world but you wants to move forward, someone will surely knock down the last gate blocking the road."

With that, I stand up and leave the room. There is nothing more I can do. The decision is his. All I can do is hope that he makes the right one.

· 17 ·
Waiting
Washington, DC

Brynn and I silently speed walk back to the car, not sure whether the president will have us followed or not. Reaching it, we get in and speed away.

"You heard everything?" I ask.

"I did. The microphone worked perfectly. And no one ever even looked my way. They have no idea."

"Good," I tell her. "We may need that later."

"How do you think it went?"

"It's hard to say, really. I think he understands that this could change the world. I think he believes. But I don't think he wants to give up control."

"I know, I was thinking the same thing. What now?"

"Now, we head back to the NASA building and

check in on their progress. Then we wait."

"I hate waiting," Brynn responds.

"I know, so do I. But we don't really have a choice."

"I know," she says. "I just wish there was something more we could do."

"I think I've done all I can, for now, hun. It's really up to him now."

We arrive at the NASA building and walk inside. We find the men sitting down talking, smiles on their faces. They light up even bigger when they see us.

"How'd it go?" asks Simon, excitedly.

"It's hard to say, yet. I said what I needed to say. Now we just have to wait for a decision."

"Well, at least we have good news," he tells me.

"What's that?" I ask.

"We determined that the metal is not something that can be made from materials on Earth. And none of the other items are able to be made here either. Not with the technology we currently have, at least."

"Well, I'm glad we have legitimate scientific backing now," I say to Brynn. "But what happened to texting me?"

"We only just finished. We were celebrating when you came in."

"Aah, okay. No worries," I tell him. "It wouldn't have mattered today anyways. So we can collect our things now?"

"Yes, yes. We're done with them. There is nothing more we can do until we have more time and better equipment."

We place everything back in the bag after I take inventory, making sure everything is there. Leaving the building, the ex-Director shuts and locks the door behind us. "Keep that key," I tell him. "Never know if you'll need it again or not."

We say our goodbyes, Brynn and I each thanking them for their help. I remind them that I may be needing them again soon, and ask them to keep in contact.

Turning to Simon, I ask, "Would you like to stay with us tonight? We have a spare room. We'd enjoy treating you the same way you did us.

"I'd love to," he replies. "I can't say no to a home cooked meal. I don't really want to make the eight-hour flight again anyways."

"Deal then. Let's go turn this rental car in and head home before it gets too late."

We say goodbye one more time, and start driving. On the way, Simon can't quit talking about the amazing properties of the items they got to study. Metal densities and strength, the odd glass, even the colors. He went into extreme detail, occupying most of the ride home with his excitement.

When we finally walk into the front door, I'm just as glad to be home as I was the last time I found myself here. It looks like the police hadn't gotten around to searching it yet, either. That would have been a disaster.

After I show Simon to his room, we begin working

on dinner. The small talk is nice, and feels necessary as we all wait to hear something from the president.

Once we've eaten, it becomes obvious that we won't hear anything tonight. We decide to head for bed, all wanting to rest after the long day we've had. *I'm sure we'll need energy for tomorrow,* I think. *These last few days have been busy.*

··●··

The next morning, I awaken to the smell of breakfast being cooked. I look over and see Brynn still in bed with me. I get dressed and walk out to the kitchen and find Simon cooking away.

"Good morning!" he says happily. "I love breakfast, and I thought I'd cook you two something nice for your hospitality."

"Thanks," I tell him, surprised.

Brynn walks out of the bedroom, and they have about the same conversation. I get on the computer to check my social media accounts that have been neglected for a day.

I accept the friend requests I have gotten, and see that the protests still haven't stopped. *Good.* I'm going to need every bit of help I can get.

Remembering the list of senators I created a few days ago, I have an idea. *Time for another mass email,* I think to myself. I add in the first email address, and start typing.

"My name is Ira Sanders. I am the man the president was looking for, and the man behind the social media posts. Everything you have seen is real. I now have four scientists from two countries that can verify this.

What you don't know is that I had a meeting with the president yesterday. I gave him information regarding where I got the items in my pictures, and why I brought them here. I told him where the world could be if he would make a few changes.

I am emailing you today to ask you to help me push him in the right direction. I know how hard you fought to keep him from doing the things he did to this country. I need you to fight just as hard now. The world needs your help.

I cannot fill you in on all of the details. But what I can tell you is that if we can get the president to do what we request, the world will forever change for the better.

The major thing I need you to ask for is the removal of the walls. Next is the firewalls blocking international communication. Also, we need to push for his endorsement in ending pollution and famine.

I know this seems like a lot. It is. But don't think it will come as a shock when you ask him. He has already heard the same from me. In an effort to convince you, I will tell you this. If these changes are made, the world will follow suit. And when it does, we will become more advanced than you ever thought possible, through the people who gave me the technology you have seen.

Thank you for your consideration and help. Other senators who fought against the president's changes will be receiving this email as well.

For verification of what I have told you, I have attached a recording of a meeting between myself and the president. I hope you find it useful. I sure did. Take care,

Ira Sanders"

I blind carbon copy all of the other senators and send the message.

Over breakfast, I tell Brynn and Simon what I did. They both support the decision. Just as I thought earlier, "Every bit helps," Brynn says.

"Have you thought of anything we can do?" asks Simon.

"I haven't," I tell them. "I really don't know what else to do besides wait. I know it sucks, but I feel like I have honestly done everything I can."

"What about meeting with France and Switzerland while we wait?" Brynn says. "Simon already warned them, so they might be willing to meet us on short notice."

To Simon, I ask, "How soon do you think we could get a meeting with them?"

"I think we could do it as soon as you are able," he replies. "They were eager when I talked to them last. I'm sure even more so now."

"Let's do it, then. We don't need to wait for the president. We can get the rest of the world on board while he makes his decision."

"I think that's a good idea," Brynn tells me. "There's no need to wait."

"Simon, can you make a call? And we'll need to use your plane again, if that's okay."

"Of course," he says. "I'll need to get it home somehow anyway."

We spend the rest of the day, and most of the night, traveling. Driving, flying, and driving some more. Eating on the road, and barely getting any rest. *It's worth it, though,* I tell myself as I lay my head down on the pillow in Simon's guest bed. Each day brings us closer to a decision.

After another Simon-cooked breakfast, I log in to my email. I have emails from multiple senators, all saying they'll help. They all say that they will push the president as hard as they can, and enlist others to do so as well. I reply with a quick message of thanks and log back off.

Simon gained a lot of ground yesterday. He was able to get me a meeting with both France and Switzerland today, and convinced Italy and Germany to come to Geneva for the meeting as well. No one else could make it on such short notice. There will be plenty of time to meet the rest of the world leaders later.

Unfortunately, there's not much time today, and Brynn and I are nowhere near ready. Thankfully, Simon takes us to a local clothing store, where Brynn and I each pick out some new clothes. We need something professional, since we didn't bring anything like that with us. I get a few suits while Brynn gets a few dresses.

Returning home, we quickly change. We don't have much time before our meeting. I grab my bag as we walk out the door.

We arrive at the CERN headquarters with about fifteen minutes to spare. We get inside, and find the room Simon said would be good for the meeting. Sure enough, it is perfect. There is no podium. I don't want that. It has a giant round wooden table, with seats all the way around. Perfect for me to address everyone not as a position of authority, but as an equal. Brynn and I stand at the door and wait for everyone else to arrive while Simon tells the people in the lobby where to send our guests when they get here.

Switzerland arrives first, naturally, and shakes our hand before taking a seat. France and Germany come in at about the same time, again greeting us kindly before walking into the room. Italy shows up last, but still not late, and takes their seat after thanking us for asking them to join.

Without wasting time, I get started. I introduce Simon as one of the scientists who has already studied the items. Before I pull anything out of my bag, though, I tell them about my experience. I explain to them what the men aboard the Zavilisk taught me about the universe, and what it means for those of us on Earth. I then told them what I was brought on board for, and why they think I can help.

I also went into great detail explaining what we need to do in order to join this universal community. When I saw the concerned looks on their faces, I explained my reasoning.

"While yes, this does seem like a difficult task, I know it is all possible. The people of Earth have no problem coming together as one when we need to. They have already. All we need to do is give them direction. Show them how to help, and how to make the changes we need to make. I have no doubt they will do it willingly. And ending war will come naturally. There is nothing to fight over when we begin our new life as one group instead of many. No need to fight when we exist as just a small part of the universe, instead of as a large part of Earth. We can make this happen. All it takes is cooperation and collaboration."

Thankfully, they consider this for a minute, then all agree. *This is going to be much easier than with our president,* I think.

I pull the items from my bag and pass them around the table, now that they have all agreed to do their part. They are all amazed at these wonders of technology. They ask what some are, and I give a demonstration. With the holographic screen, I pull up the video feed of the ship and describe what they are seeing. I also explain how the device works. I then explain the silicon life form and describe the environment it lives in. I go over the space dust as well, turning out the lights so that they can see the light that comes from within. It finally feels like I am getting somewhere.

Finally, I ask them to help me. I need them to advocate to the other countries around the world. We need a meeting between them all, preferably here in Geneva. I tell them again how important all of this is, and what it could mean for our future. They agree, and we plan for a meeting four days from now in Geneva.

Once the room is empty, we head back to Simon's house. He offers for us to stay there with him until the meeting in four days, and we decide to do it. He's friendly, and we can continue planning until then. It doesn't hurt that he cooks well, either.

There is only one thing I can't seem to get out of my head. We still haven't heard from the president. I don't know what to make of it. By now, he should have either called for my arrest and had someone chase me down, or acknowledged that the world needed to change, and began removing the many changes he put in place. Nothing has happened, though. Not a single thing. Silence.

"I don't know what to make of it," Brynn says.

"I really don't either," agrees Simon. "Like you

said, he isn't really necessary, but it would be nice to see him make the changes on his own."

"I know," I tell them. "I don't know what to make of it. And I hate waiting. We've only got four days before we meet the rest of the world on this issue. He better come up with something on this before then, or it may not go so well for him afterward."

And I mean it. I know that if the rest of the world agrees, this will happen regardless. We *are* moving forward. I'd just hate to see the president removed from power just to make it happen, no matter how much I dislike him. *We will see,* I think. *He's running out of time.*

·18·
The World Stage
Geneva, Switzerland

THE next three days crept by, with nothing to do but wait. We kept up with social media, and were happy to see that the protests remained peaceful. I popped in occasionally, just to show that I'm still around, and to motivate everyone to stay peaceful. I also left a teaser that something big was happening in a few days.

As the meeting date grew closer, we all became more and more anxious. Simon cooked more, and we all talked about the meeting, and what I will say, until we couldn't talk about it anymore. Day and night for three days, it is nearly all we talked about.

We picked a venue almost immediately. For convenience, we decided on the Palexpo. It is near the airport and has vast amounts of space. It is also quite beautiful inside, and Simon was able to get it for us on short notice. We sent emails to all parties involved, who then sent out emails to other countries that they thought would be interested in attending.

Really, we currently have no idea who might be attending. The potential numbers are high, but that doesn't mean that they will all attend. It's a guessing game until the time comes.

That time is now.

We scrambled all morning to prepare, ensuring that everything was as close to perfect as possible. Simon has so many contacts within the scientific community, we had virtually unlimited resources at our disposal. We had display cases installed to house the items I brought. Everything is in place except the radio, which will stay with me.

The holographic screen is operating, showing a live feed of the cockpit area of the ship. The lighting above the glass cube of space dust is turned off, allowing the light from within to shine outward. The piece of metal is on a pedestal so that it may be touched, adding to the experience. The canister and jar containing the silicon specimen are in one display, but separated so that each may be seen. And a video camera is facing each item, wired to a projector so that they may all be viewed from anywhere in the room.

Chairs have been set up for seating, and a podium is on the stage for me. The fours scientists I have enlisted for help have seating beside me on stage, so that they may answer any questions after my speech.

We even set up a video camera. The entire meeting will be recorded, and each country will be given a video to distribute or hold as they see fit.

No seating has been specifically designated for anyone else, and this is not without reason. The desired result of all of this is a unified world, where there are no borders or wars, no difference between people. No more upper class or lower class, and no one is any more important than anyone else. So it seems to fit that all of the seating is the same, and people have to mingle together. *Get used to it,* I think.

As I stand behind the podium, watching the last few stragglers file in, the seriousness of my situation hits me. I am about to speak to the entire world. Even the Pope has come to hear me out. My job is to convince them to accept this new future as their own. I have written a speech for today, but that in no way means that I am prepared to deliver it. The task seems daunting, but Brynn and Simon have assured me that I can do it. My confidence wavers at times, but the necessity outweighs my nervousness.

Finally, the last few people take their seats. There are far more people here than I ever imagined would actually come. Nearly every country is represented. The room is filled with a quiet murmur, whispered greetings from people who have never or rarely met. The majority of the world's leaders sit before me, some of whom brought high-ranking cabinet members along with them. It's difficult just to interrupt these powerful men and women, let alone address them with a speech. *But,* I remind myself, *they won't be this powerful for long.*

"Hello," I say, beginning. The silence envelops me completely, the world suddenly giving me all of their attention. "I am Ira Sanders, and I am here today to tell you what is to come of this world, if we let it. You can call me a liaison if you wish. I described myself like that just the other day. When the shoe fits, right? I am going to tell you both possibilities we face right now, and by the end, the correct choice should be apparent. Thank you all for coming, and I hope you are prepared for the future.

"First, I want to ask that you hold all questions until the end. I will be telling you everything I know. Next, I'll give you a fact. Keep this in the back of your head while you listen. It's rather important. They want us to join them. Now, I'll start at the beginning.

"These men brought me aboard their ship not with the intention of experimenting like you see in movies and conspiracy theories, but with the intention of educating me.

"They taught me about the universe, and about how they operate. They taught me history, and there's a lot more to it than the creation of Earth. They taught me about their ship, and about the technology that is showcased today. Everything I could possibly learn in three days, they taught me. And I am going to teach you, as much as I can. More could follow depending on the path we choose.

"In the beginning, it was one advanced species

that first made deep space travel possible. They traveled the universe, and eventually came upon another planet that had signs of life. They made contact and gained intelligence from each other. The first advanced species enabled the second to join their level. They then decided to continue this act, finding species that are advanced enough to understand and do the same.

"Eventually, they created a council. This council decided to create rules that governed when they would contact a brink species, a species that is close to meeting the standards. Once they made contact, they would teach them, and enable them to join them in space. This process still continues today.

"The rules are simple. There is no war within the universe. None at all. It may seem surprising, considering what life on Earth has been like. But rest assured this is a normal process for developing species. However, since nothing but peace exists within the universe, they expect peace on the potential planets as well. No war. None. So simple, yet so hard. The next rules are a little easier. A plan must exist to eliminate pollution and famine. It is understood that these cannot be accomplished in a day, and it is not expected to be done before contact is made. Lastly, we are to come together as one species. This is the one I originally thought to be the hardest, but I believe I was incorrect. I will elaborate shortly.

"Once these stipulations are met, contact would be made. They come to our planet. Teach us their ways, and give us all available information. They show us how to build, operate, and understand all of the technology that they have. They would enable us to join them.

"After teaching us about the universe, they would then ask us to form a council of our own. World leaders, like yourselves, and scientists, among many others, are to come together. The expectation is for you all to lay out the facts, and decide whether universal expansion is right for Earth at this moment.

"If you decide that we are ready, then the process starts immediately. They aid us in attaining space travel and reaching their level of advancement.

"If you were to decide that we are not ready, then they give us a single piece of technology and leave. They leave us with a means of communicating with them. Should you eventually decide that we are ready, you are to use the communication device to tell the council, and they will immediately dispatch a ship to come work with us. The idea is that either way, eventually, they are able to welcome us to the community.

"This is what they call it. A universal community. Can you imagine? Unlimited potential. Nowhere is too far. Vacationing on a distant planet, or inviting your other-worldly friends over for the weekend. Nothing is out of reach. That possibly is so close, you can almost feel it now, isn't it?

"The other species throughout the universe are very much like us. Since most planets that are in the habitable zone contain the same basic elements, most carbon based life followed roughly the same evolutionary path that we did. We may look a little different, with longer or shorter appendages, or higher noses, but we are also very much the same.

"The same, except for one thing. The reason they are so adamant about us joining them. We, humans, have a trait that is so normal to us, it goes unnoticed. But to others, it is a mystery. The ability to come together as one at will, and to do anything to help our fellow man.

"I know, I know, I sound like a madman. But break it down. It's true. Look at the world's reaction after a terror attack or natural disaster. Massive amounts of people from every walk of life come together to provide aid.

"And doing anything to help our fellow man. Consider that for a second. It happens every day. Pushing a car from the path of an oncoming train. Jumping onto a subway track to assist a fallen passenger. Walking into a burning building to pull someone out, with no surety that they will even be alive when you get there. Hell, people flood their systems with massive amounts of adrenaline and pull cars off of others. The fact is, this does happen, all the time. And we don't even see it.

"These are not common traits throughout the universe. In fact, they are almost solely human based. The hope is that through viewing us, and learning from our actions, it can eventually become common universe wide. Think about it. Your ship suddenly loses its oxygen supply, and someone from another supercluster shows up to aid you. If the possibilities were endless before, they are infinite now.

"Now, let me explain the alternative life forms found throughout the universe, and then I'll dive into some of the technology.

"There is other life, besides carbon-based life. Scientists here on Earth have hypothesized that this may be the case, but they surely never expected what we see before us now. While this creature is unusual and frankly, ugly, it is relatively harmless. It has no interest in entering your body or eating you. It just exists, for no apparent reason. Those creatures travel in swarms, like bees. There are only two real dangers, and both are minute. One is that a few of them could get caught in an air intake, but most ships have measures in place to prevent that. The other would be a massive swarm blocking your vision. The other defense against this is to just stay away. They don't normally travel far from planets that are uninhabitable from us, which means we have no reason to be near them anyways.

"Now, technology. I know, you've been waiting for it. I'll start with what you can't see. The ships use an intriguing method to bring people aboard while they're in the air. They can be anywhere in the universe, as long as they have your coordinates. It is safe for me to tell you because it is so far out of our reach. It involves the use of dark matter, and creating a tunnel through it. The same process is used to move throughout the universe. Basically, your existence ends in one place at the same time it begins in another.

"They are able to manipulate light in somewhat of the same way. There is not a single lightbulb on the ship. The light just exists, and is mostly controlled by motion. I cannot tell you how it works because I do not know.

"The hologram you see there is currently displaying a live video feed of the cockpit area of the ship. The terminals you see to the left and right are the navigation areas, where crew members keep track of the location and keep the ship on track. The area in the front is the cockpit. It looks as if Alter, the Captain, is there now.

"The hologram itself is simple. It is pre-programmed with specific channels, which can then be by swiping your hand from left to right across the screen. The bar at the bottom is basically the computer, display driver, and energy source all in one. It can be paired with normal computer items, like a keyboard or mouse, or it can be used as a touchscreen device.

"The metal is a product that we have no capability of producing on Earth. We just do not have the correct elements. We could have access to them, though, if we play our cards right. It is extremely lightweight, and exceptionally strong. Stronger than anything we have today.

"You've seen the canister and creature. What you do not know yet, though, is that even at such a light weight, the canister can be sealed airtight and still not crumple in the extreme pressures of space.

"The item that is most special to me is the glass cube. It was given to me as a gift. This cube contains dust particles from the center, the real center, of the universe. Those are the oldest particles anyone has ever seen, not just humans. The light in the center was not placed there by an advanced species, either. It is just a part of the particles. The extreme moments of creation caused both light and matter to become one.

"The last bit of technology I can tell you about today is the radio I have right here. It is not large, and very nondescript. It looks almost like it's just a hunk of steel right? Wrong. It can broadcast a radio signal to any compatible receiving device throughout the universe. The hologram can't even do that. And the voices you hear on the other end are clearing than talking on your cell phone. I can, and have, used this device to contact the people on the ship.

"The ship that, by the way, is waiting inside the Milky Way galaxy for us to make a decision. They are that certain themselves that we are ready. A little bit of pressure? Yeah. Can we handle it? Of course. We're humans. Apparently, we can handle anything."

· 19 ·
A Noble World
Geneva, Switzerland

I PAUSE for effect, letting my message sink in. *They need to understand the stakes. Need to feel it.* When I think the time is right, I jump into the next part of my speech.

"So let's talk about Earth. The problems we face, what we can do, and our road ahead. The issues seem huge, I know. But we can break it down. I've got the big picture. It's been in my head since day one of my journey. But you don't. I'm going to put it there for you.

"War. Scary topic, right? No. It's not that complicated. Just don't do it. If we decide to make this great leap, it will be too easy. There is no need for war when we are one people. We won't be the US, France, Russia anymore. We'll be Earth. So there is no need to fight for land. It's everyone's land. There's plenty more throughout the universe if we need it. There are plenty of planets that can host life but currently don't.

"And as one people, what else can we not do? We can't hate! We are all the same! We already are. We always have been. Some people just struggle to see it. But now, seeing that there are millions of other species out there, it makes silly problems like skin color go away. We actually are the same, in comparison to those outside of Earth.

"The entire universe is peaceful, people. The whole thing. If trillions and trillions of species can get along, Why in the hell are we still struggling to do it on Earth. Maybe this is just the eye-opener we need.

"Famine. Too easy as well. Feed everyone! There are countries that are so rich in food they don't know what to do with it all. Yes, that's right, you know who you are. Quit hoarding food! We should be disappointed in ourselves for letting it get this bad to begin with. Sure, humanitarian organizations do what they can, but that's not enough. We can fix this just by sharing what we have already.

"With the number of planets in the universe, I'm sure there are some used for food production as well. We could make greenhouses on moons if we wanted. The possibilities are endless. There is absolutely no reason for anyone to go hungry anymore. With this change, we will no longer have an excuse for starvation.

"Okay, pollution. This one is actually much

simpler than you might expect, as well. There are tons of products out there to help clean up the oceans. Even more startup companies with great ideas just waiting on funding to make them a reality. We can clean the oceans in no time.

"And trash on land? Throw it away and recycle! I was in the military. I've been deployed. I know what some of you do with your trash. It doesn't belong on the side of the road, guys, come on. I'm not saying that the US is any better. There are plenty of lazy people that won't walk three feet to a trash can. But we can fix this. You know it. I know you do.

"Famine and pollution were pushed to the bottom of the barrel. I get it. There have been much more important things to deal with, like national debt and income inequality. War and defense spending take up large portions of budgets as well. It was understandable, to a point. Those were easy subjects to ignore, since they never directly affected anyone in this room. But not anymore. We can agree today to end funding for war and defense. Release that money and use it for these special projects. We don't need defense spending anymore anyway, right?

"Now, there's one more topic I'd like to talk about, and I'm going to use it to tie everything together. Hang in there guys and gals, the time for questions will be here soon.

"Resources. I know, it's a whopper. Whether we want to admit it or not, it is a huge cause of war and land disputes. But that's old news! I can fix it. There is one thing about space that I failed to mention earlier. There is a method to my madness, though. Throughout the universe, there are trillions of planets that are not habitable. Scientists have already told us this. What they didn't know, though, is that the advanced species use these planets to their advantage. They mine them.

"That's right. There are mining operations ongoing on countless inhospitable planets. Whatever resources are available are taken for our use. There are even planets used solely for growing things. Edible things. See where I'm going here? And these planets used for mining have every element known to man. In vast quantities. This would be available to us as well. More resources than we could ever use in our lifetime. Maybe even in Earth's lifetime.

"But that's not even the best part. Let me tell you. Hold onto your armrests, this one is a doozy. It's all free. Yep. There is not a thing in the entire universe that costs money to use.

"Fuel sources are limitless. This is mostly because it's just atoms and science stuff, but that's beside the point. Building materials are limitless. Water is available in large amounts as well. To boil it down even further, this means that our potential is limitless. We can go anywhere. Do anything. And it doesn't cost a penny to do it.

"To bring that back down to a smaller scale, it also means that nothing on Earth would cost anything either. I know you were thinking I was crazy there for a while, but it's not so crazy now, is it? We can end pollution, hunger, and war so easily because *it won't cost us a damn thing to do it.* Food is free. Materials are free. So land is free. Why fight over a resource that is scarce on Earth when there is an entire planet made of it two galaxies over? And when we can travel as they can, that's practically like going next door to ask your neighbor for some butter.

"So now that I've revealed the big secret, I'll leave you with this. We humans have known for a long time that we were meant for space travel. We didn't know how, and we didn't know when. But we have known that we wanted to reach the final frontiers of space. That is a reality now, if we will allow it. The choice is ours, of course. No one is forcing us to do anything. But I personally can't find a single reason not to go for it.

"Before we start the questions, though, I want to invite a very special guest. He's not here, I'm afraid. Though if you'd let him, he could be very soon. Let me introduce you to Kalis, the Chief Scientific Officer aboard the Zavilisk, the ship that started this journey for us all.

"Kalis, are you there?" I ask, picking up the radio. The screen fills with the live video of the ship.

"I'm here, my friend. How are things going, Ira?"

The world is stunned. While they have may have now come to expect the unexpected, this is over the top. They are now seeing and hearing the voice of an alien. The room booms even louder than before, with shouts of surprise and excitement.

"Please, calm down," I beg. "Everyone will get a chance to speak with him and ask questions shortly."

Turning my attention back to the radio, I say, "Well, Kalis, I'm in the middle of a meeting with just about every world leader, if that tells you anything. We'd like to see you. I'm sure everyone has some questions as well."

"Of course, of course. I'd love to help. Give me just a minute. Are you watching the cockpit live?

"We are," I say, watching the faces in the crowd slowly become filled with awe.

"Okay, I will be there shortly."

"We'll be waiting, Kalis. Thank you."

Looking to the crowd, I tell them, "Well, if there are any questions you'd like to ask me personally, now is the time to do it."

The room bursts into noise, with everyone trying to get their question out at once. *I didn't quite plan this far*, I think.

"Please, please, one at a time! Here, we have an extra microphone. Simon, do you mind passing it out to those with the most productive or intriguing questions?"

"Sure," he replies, smiling. Happy to help, he climbs from the stage. The room is still roaring as he finds our first person. Finally, he stops.

"The first question is one that everyone is going to want to ask," Simon says. "So I figured I would get it out of the way first." Passing the microphone off, the first question comes.

"What was it like on the ship?"

"The ship was amazing. Life was simple. My room contained only a bed, with a restroom attached. Everything was metal. They provided me with everything I needed.

"The food was very basic, but it contained all of the life-sustaining properties we require. It had no smell, and very little taste. It had the consistency of oatmeal, but it was pleasant. Definitely edible.

"Every day, after eating, we went to the most amazing room. It was enormous, with a vaulted ceiling that was easily as tall as the room we are in now. There were a number of different stations in the room, some with computers, and others with servers. In the front of the room was by far the best part, though. The entire front wall was nothing but windows. From here, I could see part of the ship, as well as space.

"And that view of space is awe inspiring. Never have I seen something so beautiful. It is so black, I can't even describe it. The absence of light is something that everyone should experience. And then, just when you thought the blackness would go on forever, there was the tiniest pinprick of a star or galaxy. It truly is an amazing sight.

"I was only there for a few days, but I could never forget my time there. I look forward to the day that I can go back."

Simon senses the end of my answer, and moves on to the next person.

"What is different about the people aboard the

ship? Like, physically."

"Well, their eyes are all the same color and farther apart than ours. Their noses are longer. Their lips are thin and their ears sit higher on their heads. And their skin is kind of grey, and almost translucent."

"What made them decide to choose you," asked the next person.

"That's something personal, and I'd rather not discuss it," I tell him.

"Why did they choose now?" came the next.

"They have actually been studying us for quite a few years," I begin. "They were close to making contact before the US president made the changes he made. Originally, they were going to leave and return again, at least half of a century from now. But they decided that because of the special trait we possess, it may be beneficial to have a citizen attempt to steer us in the right direction. That's where I came in."

"Where is the US, anyway? Why isn't your president here?"

"President Jacobs has already heard most of this information," I tell them as the room immediately roars. "But this was not out of choice on my part. If I did not give him some information, I would have been thrown in jail or worse. I had no other option. Trust me, he has plenty to figure out on his end. Soul searching, if you will."

About that time, Kalis appears in the video screen. "Hello again, Ira," he says.

"Hey, Kalis. These people have some questions

for you. Do you mind answering what you can?

"Of course not. Ask away."

The first question comes immediately. "How do you move through space? I understand the process Mr. Sanders explained, but how much time does it take?"

"Well," Kalis begins, "Moving long distances through the use of our matter distributor is essentially instant. I'm sure Ira explained that much to you. However, this process takes up large amounts of energy. Fuel is limitless, but space aboard the ship is not. So, using the matter distributor is inefficient to use for short distances. This is alleviated by the speed at which our engines can move a ship, though. The use of nuclear and laser power, and the addition of the technology that we have, can make trips from one star system to the next take mere hours, in the same galaxy."

"Can you tell us more about the council?" asks a female voice.

"The council consists of twenty members, ranging from species that have barely joined the community to those that have been advanced for billions of years. They are lenient, as Ira could tell you. As long a species can show a solid plan to better themselves, and a complete elimination of war, they are willing to teach them the ways of the universe. Keep in mind, too, that we would be there to assist you with your planning."

"What about the council on our planet? What does that consist of?"

"The council on your own planet," Kalis starts, "consists of whoever you think needs to be there. I would advise scientists of multiple disciplines, psychologists to assess the changes in the population, and of course the world leaders. I believe Ira has already enlisted the help of four scientists, so they should be there since they have already established a baseline. And Ira himself, since he has the most experience with us."

Someone else asks, "How are you able to control light?"

"That is a question I cannot answer at this time. If and when you choose to join the community, you will be made aware of the technology that allows us to do that."

"How can we be sure this isn't fake?" comes from the back of the room.

"Ask the scientists," Kalis replies.

"This is definitely not fake," Simon cuts in. "We studied the technology you see before you thoroughly, and it is all very real. The metal doesn't contain a single element that is found on Earth. And there is nothing like that creature, fossilized or live, that has ever existed on our planet. It's silicon-based. There is nothing like that here. I can assure you, ma'am, that this is as real as it gets."

The questions keep pouring in, and the scientists are eventually able to join in and answer more. They cover every possible subject, some of which I even covered myself already. After over an hour, it has finally died down.

"Okay, Kalis, I think you can get back to work now," I tell him.

"Thank you for allowing me to help," he responds. "And thank you for the educated and well thought out questions. I'll speak to you soon, Ira. Take care."

I turn back to the room, and we begin a discussion on where to go from here. The world is surprisingly open minded. Most have already fervently voiced their opinion. They want change. They want possibility. And they want to see what the universe has to offer.

However, they have also decided that even though we are closed off from the world, the United States needs to be heard from. Something of this magnitude cannot be done without the agreement of all parties involved. Meaning, the world.

I explain that the president is aware of the facts, and has many advisors assisting him in coming to a conclusion. They still will not budge with their opinion. The US is too powerful to make a decision like this without them. Too much destruction could be had should the president decide that he disagrees.

It is obvious now. With both noble and security-conscious reasons winning out, their minds are made up. The world will not falter in their resolve. No decision will be made without the opinion of President Jacobs.

· 20 ·
Choices
The White House

"HE invited the leaders of every country but me?!" the president shouted, looking just as angry as ever. He whirls around the office as if looking for something to throw.

"To be fair, would you have really gone and remained objective?" asks the vice president, visibly worried that he will, in fact, throw something.

"It doesn't matter if I would have gone or not. I didn't even know it was occurring!"

"Well, it's behind us now. Let's keep moving forward. There is nothing we can do about the past. What can we do currently?"

"There's not a damn thing we can do about it now. You're right, Jim. Is there even a video or audio recording? Anything? We need to know what they know."

"I'll have someone start looking," the vice president replies. "There is one other thing we can do as well."

"What's that?"

"Join the rest of the world in their decision."

"Out of the question. Just get him on the phone after you find someone to look for a recording."

"Who, sir?"

"Sanders, of course. I need to speak with him again. This has got to stop."

"On my way," the vice president replies, walking out the door. *I swear he's losing it. I've never seen him this flustered before.*

President Jacobs paces, circling the desk. Still fuming, he thinks, *I don't know what Sanders is thinking, but no one has ever disrespected me this way. He's not going to get away with it.*

His phone beeps, letting him know that there is a call waiting. *Better be him.*

Picking it up, he immediately hears, "Hello, Mr. President."

"How'd you know it was me?"

"Well, when the operator says, 'Please hold for the president,' I get a pretty good feeling I know who is on the other end."

"Alright, smart ass. Let's get one thing straight. You will *not* speak to me however you like. I am the president, and I deserve your respect."

"I give my respect to those who have earned it.

In your case, I'm already giving you more than you deserve."

"Enough! Tell me what you talked about in the meeting you didn't invite me to."

"Oh, that's what this is about? I should have guessed it. You already know most of it. The rest, you should have been there for. They had a pretty good experience you missed out on."

"I would have been there if I would have been invited!" the president yells, waving for the vice president to sit as he walks through to door.

"I told you, the world won't wait. If you would be more receptive to change, you would have been there right along with everyone else. And how was I supposed to invite you when your firewalls prevent me from contacting you?"

"Drop the lies, Sanders. I know you can communicate with the states. I've seen your posts."

"I don't know what you're talking about, Mr. President. You wouldn't be trying to coerce me into admitting guilt, would you?"

"Don't change the subject, Sanders. What did you show them?"

"Oh, they got to see everything, up close and personal. Walk among the things I brought back. Touch them and explore them. They even got to have a conversation with a member of the ship."

"You let them see the items? *And* they spoke to a member of the ship?!"

"Of course, I did. They haven't threatened to

take them and throw me in jail like you have. I have nothing to hide from them."

"I swear, Sanders, I am going to make an example of you when we find you. And we will find you."

"Hard to find a man that is currently being offered refuge by every European nation," Ira tells him. "I tell you what. You come to your senses and agree to make some changes, and I'll let you see everything just like everyone else."

"I'm going to see everything regardless."

"I think this is one of those 'easy way versus the hard way' moments, sir. It would be a lot easier for all involved if you'd just get on board with the rest of the world."

"I don't care what's easier! I care about bringing you down, and making this country stronger."

"You won't be bringing anyone down, soon."

"What the hell is that supposed to mean?" President Jacobs asks.

"Exactly what I said. The world isn't going to wait forever. Their leaders decided to wait on you. They don't want to make a decision without your input. But that doesn't mean the people will wait. And the leaders won't wait forever, either."

"They can keep waiting, for all I care. It's going to be a while. Like two more years, at least. And that's only if someone runs against me in the next election and manages to win."

"Oh, I'm sure it won't be that long. Like I said, the public won't wait. They'll be beating down your door before you know it. And if they start taking it out on their own governments as well, all bets are off. Those nations will do anything at that point," Ira tells him.

"None of what you told me will ever really work anyways," he tells me.

"Oh it can, and it will. Ask any other person that was there. They will all tell you that my plan would work perfectly. And it wouldn't cost us a dime."

"Now you're just being ridiculous. I told you, quit with the lies. I don't care what you say, Sanders, I will not lose control of this country."

"Okay, Mr. President. I'm going to go now. I'm tired of the constant back and forth with you. Should I remind you of what else I said last time? Time is running out to save what's left of that reputation of yours. And what's left is already wearing thin as well. If you don't act soon, there will be nothing left to save."

"I'll worry about my own damn reputation, thank you."

"Well, you better start soon. Goodbye, Mr. President."

The president slams the phone down on the receiver, nearly hard enough to break it.

"He's right, you know," the vice president reminds him. "You really do need to start thinking about what is to come."

"That doesn't mean I need to do it his way!" the president shouts, spinning his chair around and jumping up.

"True, but his way may be the only way at this

point. He really seems to have a good grasp on this. He would have made one hell of a politician, honestly."

President Jacobs glares at him, angered at just how right the vice president is. "I meant what I said, Jim. I'm not going to give up the control that I have."

"Sir, we've even got senators calling for you to give in. United States senators. Sanders has everyone in his pocket. If their constituents find out, they'll be applying even more pressure, and more senators will join them. This thing can snowball quickly. It's already started."

"Those senators don't matter. They're the same ones that lobbied against me when I was running for president. Of course they'd be against me now. But just like before, they're powerless."

"They do matter, sir. They represent the people. If the general public starts asking the senators to push harder, they will. That's their job, and they will do it, especially when they want the same thing. We can only withstand so much before we have to give in."

"I will *not* give in."

"Sir, I really don't think you have a choice anymore."

"I always have a choice."

"Not when the entire world wants you to do the opposite of what you're currently doing. Sir, if you don't make the changes the world is calling for, the people will call for an impeachment. I can see it coming now."

"They can't do that!"

"They can, sir. It's the way the system works. If you don't act in the interest of the nation, they will."

"I *am* acting in the interest of the nation. I'm the only one! I have been for the last two years!"

"That's your opinion, sir. The public's opinion is the opposite. If you fail to do what the entire United States wants you to do, they will force you out of office."

"They will do no such thing."

"The police have already let the protestors they arrested go. No one is backing you anymore. Soon there will be no one to protect you at all. You have no choice anymore, sir. Seriously. Sanders was right. They will be bursting through the door, and soon. And we have only one way to stop it."

With a knock at the door, they both turn to see an analyst walk in. "We found a video, sir," she says, handing the president a disc.

Without a word in reply, he turns his back on her and heads to his desk. As she leaves, he puts it into his computer's disc drive and presses play when the video loads.

The vice president stands beside him, bent over to see the screen. They stay that way, silently watching the world come together without them.

"My God, it really is the entire world's leaders," the vice president says in awe.

"And look at the display cases! He really did have everything there for them to see. Unbelievable."

As they listen, the vice president grows quiet.

More and more, he agrees with Ira. The world really does need this. *Imagine what it would be like,* he thinks to himself. *A world where no one hated and everyone is prosperous, just because they exist. No money, yet everything is limitless. It's amazing.*

The video ends, and they have no idea how long they've been watching for.

"Sir, I think we need to do this. In fact, I'm positive we do. He verified everything when he spoke with the man on the ship. Did you see him? It was obvious he's not human. The rest of the world has seen it too. We have to fall in line on this."

"We are doing nothing of the sort. And you will back me up. That is your job, Jim."

"Well, what do you want me to do?"

"I want that technology. All of it. And I will not stop until I get it. The rest of the world can go to hell, for all I care. They won't be able to do a thing about it once we have that stuff. We need to get Sanders. Now."

"Sir, I really don't think that's the best idea."

"I don't care, Jim. Not a bit. I am the president, and you are not. You will do what I say."

"No, I will not. I'm sorry, sir. I didn't want to have to do this, but you are impossible to reason with."

"Do what?"

Pulling out his cell phone, the vice president dials a number. When he hears a voice on the other end, he looks the president directly in the eye when he says, "You can come in now. It's time."

Immediately, the door to the oval office slams open, three FBI agents leaving distinct boot imprints on the carpet. "Mr. President, you are under arrest for treason," the lead agent says, placing President Jacobs' hands behind his back.

"This is preposterous! What in the hell do you think you're doing? I have committed no treason."

"Sir," the vice president says, a small grin now forming on his face, "according to the law you changed when you took office, treason occurs whenever a person does something that is not in the best interest of the United States. The people have spoken, and you refuse to do what the country needs. You are not above the law. So yes, you have committed treason.

"I gave you every opportunity to change your mind. I pleaded with you. The entire world did. But you have left us no choice.

"As you're well aware, I will be taking your place. So if you'll excuse me, I have a world to join."

· 21 ·
The Coup
The White House

THE Vice President spins in the chair, reveling in his victory. *It's been a long time coming,* he thinks. He sits back and puts his feet on the desk, admiring the office from a place he's never been able to sit before.

It took two years, but he was finally able to remove the man from power. *He never should have been here to begin with.* The vice president had only agreed to run after a few of the senators convinced him to. Their intention had been clear from the start. "If he wins the presidency, we need someone in office who will help us get him out," they had told him. Once the president won, he didn't contact the senators very often, for fear of being caught. It wasn't until Ira Sanders brought the world to a halt that they found a way to remove him from office, and without involving themselves publicly.

As soon as Ira had contacted the senators, the vice president had been in constant contact with them as well. *This is our chance,* he had thought. Every waking moment he was away from the president, he spent with them. They spent hours and hours planning, trying to figure out a way to bypass President Jacobs. Nothing worked. Every option, they came up with was immediately shot down by someone else, usually with good reason.

Finally, however, the vice president himself figured out a way. "Use his laws against him!" he had shouted into the phone one night in the middle of a conference call. He had remembered that the president had changed the definition of treason in the code book. After looking it up, he realized that by not doing what the overall public thought was right, he was not acting in the interests of the nation, and therefore, committing treason.

He then had every one of the senators call in every favor they had. After giving the president numerous chances to change his mind, he finally made the call. With overwhelming support, the FBI had no choice but to do it. They didn't need much motivation anyway, since most of them sided with the general population.

Change is all they wanted. Real change. Once Ira Sanders showed the world what the possibilities were, the world rose up and realized that we really are capable of getting there. The president was the only one standing in the way. *Not anymore, though.*

With that thought, the vice president decides it's time to take action. He calls for a meeting with the senators. Once the majority are on the line, he begins.

"The president is out of the way," he says, another smile forming.

The other end is instantly filled with the joyous yells of news well received. Congratulations and praise flow through to his ears, and he has a hard time fighting back the urge to join them.

"We need to work on the next step," he says, trying to reign them in.

"What is the next step?" he hears in response.

"Well, I think we need to plan before we make any kind of public announcement. This is a big deal. Not only did we remove the president from office, essentially through a coup, but we are also about to make a decision that will ultimately result in the dissolution of the United States of America, along with every other country. While it a good thing for the people of Earth, it's still a bit of a shock."

He hears numerous words of agreement from the other end, all having already come to much the same conclusion.

"So, we need to have our story straight. And a plan. We need to speak to the other nations and fill them in as well. And eventually, I think we should tell Mr. Sanders personally, instead of letting him find out through the news like everyone else. After what he's done, I think he deserves that much. It was his audio recording of the meeting he had that set this all into motion, anyway."

More agreements, and then silence again.

"How do we make an announcement? I think we should only announce the removal of the president for now. We'll need to meet with the other countries before telling the US that we are going to move forward with the plan Sanders set in motion."

"What do we tell the public, though?" one of the senators asked.

"Well, we can't outright lie. There is always someone with a video camera somewhere. Someone had to have seen him being taken away from here in cuffs."

"But they don't need to know that this was set in motion two years ago, either."

"No, no, they definitely can't know that. I think that would cast some doubt on Mr. Sanders, no matter how strong his evidence is."

"Yes, you're right. So what do we tell them?" another asks.

"Well, we can tell them that the FBI found out about some illegal trading, or some scandal," a senator throws out.

"No, I don't think that would work," the vice president says. "That's not enough. I don't think they would have immediately removed him from office because of anything like that."

"That's true," someone interjects. "Why not just the truth?"

"I think that's our best option. What he was doing was treasonous according to his law. And his actions over the last two years have been nothing less than horrendous as well. I say we go with that. Tell them that according to the law that he himself passed, he was committing treason by not doing what the entire US was asking him to do. We can even 'leak' the recording Sanders sent us," the vice president says, waiting for a response.

"The leak idea is good. Make sure it comes from an outside source, though," one of the senators replies. "We don't want that tied to us at all. Get it to a news station in some rural part of Virginia and let them release it. It'll need to come before the press release as well. Give it more legitimacy. That should have it all tied together in everyone's heads as soon as the press release comes. No one will doubt it for a second."

"We just have to make sure it doesn't get out that we had been working on this for a lot longer than Sanders has been around. This needs to be all FBI, and no one else. Besides the tipster of course."

"Yes, of course," the vice president begins. "I'll make sure none of us are tied in. I'm sure the FBI won't mind taking credit for pulling him down from his throne."

"Good. We can't have any scandal surrounding our decision to join the rest of the world. And, we don't want this council of theirs to think we aren't ready because of something like this. We don't want this thing tainted in any way."

"You're right. Now, this business of joining the world. While we all think it's a good idea, this notion is only based off of the information we have, which is all second hand. I think I'm going to bring Sanders in. I need to hear everything from him, and see the items he has myself before I can justify advocating for something like this. I think we owe the public that much."

"I understand that, and agree," one of the senators responds. "We do need to be as educated on the subject as possible."

"I wasn't there when the president met him the first time. I didn't even know the meeting was happening. If I did, I probably would have had my own man there making a recording. But, since I wasn't involved, I haven't had any direct contact with Sanders yet. I don't know how he will react to what I'm going to tell him. I'll have to somehow convince him that I am now acting as president, and acting on behalf of the nation and not myself. It may take a while to convince him, I don't know," the vice president says into the phone.

"Well, hopefully, it doesn't take too long. I don't know how much longer the world will wait."

"I know. Can one of you give me his email? I don't have any of the information on him. The president kept all of that close. I'll also need one of you to forward me the audio recording. I don't have that yet either." He writes the email down on a sticky note while someone reads it off to him, and sticks it to the center of the desk.

"Thanks, I'm going to go ahead and start on that and the press release. Keep your eyes on the TV. Everything is going to happen pretty quickly, I think. I doubt a news station will wait until evening news to let that leak go."

"Sounds good," someone replies. "We'll talk soon. That audio recording is on its way to you now."

The vice president ends the call and dials another number. "I need the press secretary in here. Now."

A woman walks through the door a few minutes later and approaches the desk. "You asked to see me, sir?"

"Yes. I just sent you an email. There is an audio recording or the president having a meeting with Ira Sanders attached. I need that sent to a rural news station and released immediately. Any station will do, just not one around here. It cannot be tied to us in any way. Set up a fake email and go to an internet café to send it if you have to. I don't care how you make it happen. Just make sure they don't know who they're getting it from. It needs to be as anonymous as possible. In fact, take one of the analysts with you. See if they can help."

"Yes, sir. Is there anything else?"

"Yes. I need you to work on a speech. We're going to do a press release later, detailing the president's crimes against the country and that he has been removed from office. Again, it cannot show my involvement in any way. Give all the credit to the FBI and refer to them for a name to tie it to."

"Not a problem sir. We'll have that done and ready soon."

"Okay. Get the audio recording sent out ASAP. I want that to spread for a bit before I conduct the press release."

"Sounds good, sir," she says, spinning on her heel and leaving the room. The door closes gently behind her, and the vice president shifts his focus to his next task.

First, he decides, he needs to find any information on Sanders the president may have left lying around. *Any insight into this man will help me with a conversation,* he thinks.

He begins with the top drawer of the desk and finds nothing but writing material. Plenty of pens, pencils, and paper, but nothing about Sanders.

Opening the next drawer down, he finds files. He pulls them out excitedly and spreads them across the desk, thinking he might have hit the jackpot. Unfortunately, it is only the daily reports he is given. Information on the weather, the war in the Middle East, and financial reports, but still nothing useful.

In the bottom drawer, he finds another file, but this one is alone. He lays it on top of the others and opens it, and finally finds what he is looking for. A detailed report on Ira Sanders. His home address, military file, phone numbers and emails, everything. All of the social media accounts are listed as well, along with a report on his recent travels. There is also a detailed report on who he has been in contact with over the course of the last week or two. On the last page is a picture of his kids. Taken from a distance, it appears the president may have been having Sanders family followed. *Just in case he could use them against him, I'm sure. How long has it been since he's seen his kids? He never should have had to sacrifice so much.* Tearing the picture up and throwing it out, he makes a mental note. Never underestimate the power of fear.

He finds the phone number for Sanders' cell phone, and types the numbers into his own. He saves it as a contact, then sets the phone on the desk. *Am I ready? I guess I don't have a choice. Hopefully, I can convince him that we are on the same side.*

With those final thoughts lingering in the back of his head, he selects the new contact and starts the call.

• 22 •
The Message
Geneva, Switzerland

IT'S the day after the meeting, and my phone is ringing for the second time already. I don't recognize the number this time, and I glance to Brynn. "I wonder who this is, now?"

She looks at the caller ID. "I have no idea. Answer it, it could be important."

Accepting the call, I put it on speakerphone. "Hello?"

"Mr. Sanders?" I hear from my hand.

"Yes," I say, intrigued. It's not often someone calls me and isn't sure who they're talking to. "Who's this?"

"This is the vice president."

Brynn's eye grow wide. "What in the hell is he calling you for?"

Beats me, I think.

"I guess you're making the president's calls for him now?" I ask.

"Not exactly," he says.

"Well, what is it then?"

"The president is out of the picture. Everything now goes through me."

I nearly drop the phone. "Please, tell me what that means," I manage to get out.

"It means that you no longer have to worry about not having the support of the white house. You didn't know it, but I had already been working with some of the same senators you contacted."

"Working with them how?"

"Can you ensure that this conversation stays between us?"

"Of course, I can," I tell him. *And Brynn, and Simon.*

"I joined his campaign with the sole purpose of taking him down if he got elected. You were the reason we were finally able to do it."

Shocked, I reply, "Wow. I wasn't expecting that. It's not often you hear about a coup in your own country. We always wondered why you ran with him, to be honest. You seemed to be his polar opposite."

"I am, on multiple levels. That's part of why I'm calling you now. I wanted you to hear it first. I want to see the items you have. Once I do, I'm going to agree to move forward with your plan. Also, make sure to keep that 'coupe' word to yourself. We don't want the public to know that's what was happening."

"Well, it's about time," I say, smiling at Brynn. "You have my word. But why do you need to see what I have? I assume you've seen the video from the meeting in Geneva by now."

"Yes, I've seen the video. However, I want to verify for myself that they're as real as you say they are. Just a video doesn't quite cut it for me."

"What about getting verification from other prominent leaders? Why don't you just speak to some of them? France, Great Britain, Switzerland, they all saw it up close. Some of them touched the things. They will tell you it's all real, sir. There's no reason to wait."

"I guess, that's true," he replies. "I'll still need to talk to them before I make anything official."

"I tell you what," I begin. "If you'll call them and set up a meeting or whatever you need to do to let them know we're moving forward, then we'll make sure that you get to see everything soon. You are one of the world leaders now, after all. You'' be right there with the rest of them, studying the new technology the ship lands."

"I'll accept that deal."

"Great! So tell me, what did you do to remove the president from power?"

"Well, the senators forwarded me the audio recording you made. That's going to be released tonight. That helped quite a bit. The reason we were able to do it, though, was because of a law he wrote himself."

"Which law was that?" I ask.

"The treason law," the vice president tells me.

"Funny, that's the same law he threatened to have me arrested over," I tell him. "How in the world did you manage to get someone to arrest him?"

"It turns out, when he refused to do what the country asked, he was violating the law himself. The FBI was on board immediately. Most of them had already decided that they agreed with you. They just needed a little nudge to get the ball rolling."

"The entire country is going to be ecstatic," Brynn says out loud.

"Yes, I'm sure they will be," he chuckles. "By the way, all of the charges against you have been dropped. You have no reason to run or hide anymore. You and your family are safe. In fact, I think you should come home. We're going to need your leadership."

"Thank you, sir. Really."

"You are very welcome, Mr. Sanders. There's one other thing I wanted to tell you. Well, maybe two."

"Go for it," I reply. "Though I don't know how much better this can get."

"You can keep the money in your account. We'll say it's for your service to the country. I know you may not need it for much longer, but until then, enjoy yourselves. Also, by the time of my press release tonight, the firewalls will be taken down. And most of the laws the president enacted will not be enforced anymore. They'll be taken off the books soon."

"That's great news, sir. Thank you again. For

everything," I reply, still amazed.

"It's no problem, Mr. Sanders."

"When will you tell the public that you're going to accept my invitation?"

"It won't be long. As soon as I speak with some of the other countries. I'll talk to you soon, Mr. Sanders. I have a lot to do."

"Okay, sir. Take care."

The call ends, and my hand drops to my side. Brynn jumps on me, tackling me with a hug and a kiss.

"You did it!" she shouts. "You actually did it."

"We did it," I say. "I couldn't have done it without your help."

Looking to Simon, I add, "And yours. Thank you, Simon."

"Don't thank me," he says. "You did all the work. I just helped with the logistics."

"Now," I say, "We still shouldn't be so excited. A lot still needs to happen."

"Like what? Brynn asks.

"Like, the world has to decide they like what they hear whenever Kalis and the rest arrive. And the council has to approve our plan to fix the world we live in now. Once all of that happens, we can celebrate. There's still a lot of work to do."

"The hardest part is over, though, thankfully. Convincing the world," Brynn replies, smiling.

"Convincing the world was done a while ago. But you're exactly right," I agree, squeezing her hand in mine. "The work is far from over, though."

"Well, until they need you again, let's do what he said. Let's go get our kids."

"Deal, I say. I've missed them."

"You and me both," Brynn replies.

"First, let's call Kalis," I decide, pulling the radio from my bag.

"Kalis?" I say, barely able to contain my excitement from bleeding through to the radio.

"Hello, my friend!" I hear after a pause. "How is it going down there?"

"I have great news," I tell him. "The US is on board. I'll be calling you again soon to tell you we're ready."

"Ira this is great news!" he says excitedly.

"I know," I reply. "I really wasn't expecting it. I figured the world would force the US into agreeing eventually, but I honestly thought it would be a couple of months, at least. But, it turns out, the vice president and some others had been planning a coupe since he took office two years ago. I happened to have given the president a reason to violate his own law."

"Well, I guess it all worked out either way. I will personally make sure you are involved in everything from now on," Kalis says. "Your family should be there as well. Now that you don't need to hide anymore, you should be with them."

"I plan on it, Kalis. You don't have to worry about that."

"How long do you think it will be before they request our presence?" he asks.

"I'm really not sure. It could be twelve hours. It could be a couple days. There's no way for me to tell you yet. I just wanted to give you a heads up. Be ready," I tell him, smiling at Brynn.

"We're ready when you are," he replies. "Take care, Ira. We'll see you soon."

"Goodbye for now, Kalis."

"Okay," I say, turning to Brynn. "Let's go get those kids." Standing up, we begin to pack our things. It seems surreal, going home after all this time.

Before we go, we spend a few minutes with Simon, thanking him.

"It's no problem," he says. "Really. If I could have done more, I would have done that as well. I am happy to have been able to help you. I'm proud to have been a part of all this."

"I'm proud to have met you," I tell him. "You'll hear from me soon. You aren't done being a part of all this yet. I won't let anything happen without you being involved."

"Thank you, Ira," he says.

"No, thank you," I say, walking opening the door. I pause for a second before closing it again. "Actually, there is one more thing you could help us with."

"Sure, anything."

"Can you give us a ride to the airport?"

··●··

We arrive home early in the morning on the next

day. Just as the vice president promised, there were no obstacles getting through security, and no one was waiting to arrest us. We pass out in bed, planning to wake back up at eight.

At nine a.m., we finally climb out of bed. We've only been asleep for a few hours, but we're ready to get the kids back. We grab some coffee and give Brynn's parents a call.

While they're on the way, I check social media one more time. I have a feeling this will be the last time I do this.

The outpouring of support is unreal. People from across the world, all with the same message: We want change. It's evident now that the entire world backs my original mission. I have no need of lobbying anymore. The rest of humanity is doing it for me.

I send a quick email to the three original scientists to let them know what is going on. Receiving an immediate reply from the ex-Director of NASA, he tells me that he saw the press release last night. I respond again, copying the other two as well, and tell them to be prepared. The world is going to need them soon.

We spend the rest of the day playing with the kids. We've all missed each other, and we definitely needed this time together. As much as I've missed them, it's hard for me to focus. I'm still waiting to hear from the vice president, or anyone else for that matter, regarding the choice they want to make.

That night, after the kids have been put to bed,

Brynn and I are finally attempting to relax for what feels like the first time in months. A new message fills our TV screen after switching to the news. I wanted an update, and I definitely got it.

"The vice president, along with the leaders of Great Britain, Germany, and every other nation in the world, have just made an announcement. Standby for another message from the vice president:

'Citizens of America, tonight I have the pleasure of bringing you good news. Along with the leaders of every other country on Earth, a decision has been made. After much deliberation, it has been decided that we will seek the support of the other-worldly species waiting in our galaxy. Like the public, we have come to the conclusion that it is time for us to drop our borders, fix the problems we have created on Earth, and join the universal community.

I want to personally thank Ira Sanders and his family for their role in this decision. Without them, none of it would have been possible.

Thank you for your time, America. Have a good night.'

That message, from our vice president. Now, back to your regularly scheduled programming."

Brynn and I stare at each other in disbelief. *It*

finally happened. After everything I've done, it's finally here. I smile and kiss my wife, both relieved and nervous at the same time.

"Let's go to bed," I say. "I'm pretty sure we're going to need our rest for tomorrow."

I check on the kids as we head to bed, glad to finally spend another night in the house with them.

Laying down, my mind wanders like it usually does. There seems to be more to rewind through every night. This time, though, it wanders to the future. A future, I realize, that is finally upon us.

Part
3
Contact

*We believe that when men reach beyond this planet,
they should leave their national differences behind
them.*

— John F. Kennedy, 21 February 1962

· 23 ·
Full Circle
Charlottesville, Virginia

THE next day, I wake up to tons of emails and missed phone calls. The senators called to congratulate me, the scientists emailed me to do the same, and the vice president had called as well, but left no message. We eat breakfast with the kids before I do anything else.

As we finish, my phone rings. I see that it's Vice President Harwell, so I answer.

"Good morning, sir," I say on speakerphone.

"Hello, Mr. Sanders," he replies cheerfully.

"I enjoyed seeing the new press release last night," I tell him. "What is our next step?"

"Well, we need to find a location for the ship to land, I suppose."

"Yes, I guess that would be rather important," I reply, surprised that I haven't thought about that yet.

"Let me do some research and I'll let you know when I figure something out. It's a massive ship. We'll need somewhere big."

"That's fine. We also need to figure out a date. I know the rest of the world is ready, so any notice is fine, as long as there is notice. I'm sure they don't want to miss the ship landing."

"Yes sir," I say. "I'm sure you're right. Have you thought about who you want on the US envoy? I know three scientists that will be involved for sure. If there's anyone else you can think of, let me know. The three that are already invited could probably give us some references, too."

"That'll be fine. See who they recommend, and we'll get them on board. I have a few psychologists in mind already. I'll contact them and bring them up to speed."

"Sounds good. I'll talk to you soon, sir."

He hangs up the phone, and I grab my computer. My kids ask who that was, and I have to fib. I don't want them to know anything until the ship lands. I think that would be the ultimate surprise. *Daddy helped bring aliens to Earth,* I laugh to myself.

"How's it feel to know what you've done?" Brynn asks. "Seeing everything almost complete must be nice."

"I'm not sure yet," I reply honestly. "The biggest thing to get used to is so many people relying on me. There's still more to do, and I'll be a big part of it all."

"I understand that," she says as I begin searching

for places large enough to land a ship of that size. Deciding on the desert, an idea hits me. It seems like the perfect place, bringing the events here on Earth full circle.

"White Sands," I tell Brynn. "That's where they should land the ship."

"Why White Sands?" she asks.

"It's the site of the first atomic bomb test," I respond. "Do you remember me telling you that I was the second person from Earth to have been brought aboard a ship like that? Well, the first person ruined it by bringing technology back with him and using it to help create the first atomic bomb."

"Oh wow, that does seem like a good place then. Is there enough space?"

"Yes, there is. It's a missile range. There's wide open desert for miles in every direction."

"I think that would be perfect, then."

"Good! That's one thing to check off of my list. Let me check in with the VP just to be sure."

Picking up my phone, I give him a quick call. After I explain the significance, he's on board one hundred percent. He says he'll call the military as soon as he gets off the phone with me, and tell them to cease operations on the base and begin preparing for the arrival. Before getting off the phone, he tells me he'll call the other world leaders and let them know, as soon as he hears from me with a date.

Ending the call, I email the scientists and ask them for recommendations on who else we should bring along. Brynn starts looking up flight plans, thinking we'll need to be there early to assist in setting everything up.

Next, I grab my radio. It's time to talk to Kalis about all of this. I can't move forward with anything else until he's caught up to speed.

"Kalis?" I ask.

"Hello, my friend!" I get in return.

"Kalis I've got big news, and I need some information from you."

"Go for it! We love good news."

"Well, let me surprise you by asking you a question. How soon can you land?"

"Ira!" he shouts. "This is amazing! We can be there anytime. All we would need is about four hours."

"Well, we don't wanna do it quite that soon," I tell him. "How about tomorrow at noon? Mountain time, if you know what that is."

"That is perfect! Where should we land?"

"That's the other thing I wanted to talk to you about. How do you feel about White Sands, New Mexico?"

"I don't know the area," he says, surprising me.

"Well, it happens to be the site of the first atomic bomb test. It's nothing but desert," I tell him, hoping for a good response.

"That sounds perfect," he tells me. "How fitting."

"That's what I thought."

"We'll look up the coordinates and be there on time," he replies.

"Deal. I'm gathering a list of scientists now. All of the world leaders will be there as well. Now, my next question. What kind of standoff distance should we have? Like, how far should everyone be the landing zone when your ship lands?"

"I think one mile would be plenty. That way we can be a little picky with adjusting for obstacles. Believe me, you'll still be able to see the ship just fine when it lands."

"Oh, I believe you. Okay, that's all for now, Kalis. Let me know when you have your exact coordinates?"

"Of course," he says. "I'll talk to you soon."

Putting the radio down, I check my email again. They have all left me recommendations, some of which are the same. I reply by thanking them and tell them to get to White Sands by noon tomorrow. I'll fill them in with more information when I get it.

With all of this done, it's time to wait. We decide to have an early lunch, and start getting the kids ready for a nap. As Brynn is laying them down, Kalis reaches me on the radio and gives me the coordinates of the location they want to use to land.

As soon as the kids are asleep, I call Vice President Harwell back.

"Mr. Sanders!" he responds, on the first ring. *This man sure is happy*, I think. Looking to Brynn, her eyes say the same thing.

"Hello, sir. I have some updates for you."

"Well let's hear it! I want to get the ball moving on this. Operations have already been shut down at the missile base."

"Great! Well, they want to land at noon tomorrow. I guess you need to hurry to let everyone know in time."

"They're all on the way here already," he tells me. "I explained the significance of the chosen site, just in case anyone was upset that it would be happening in the US. They decided to head this way immediately. No one was going to risk missing this."

I understand that," I reply. "They say we should have a standoff of about a mile. It gives them room to avoid obstacles. Kalis promised we'd be able to see the ship land no matter what." I give him the exact coordinates of their landing zone as well.

"That's fine," he tells me. He asks for the list of scientists, and I give him that too. He's satisfied, and I end the call.

We spend the rest of the day traveling. Brynn found tickets to get us to El Paso, leaving at the perfect time for us to make it to DC.

When we land, we start the long drive up to White Sands from the city. We find a hotel in Alamogordo for the night, and start working on the bedtime routine as soon as we pull in.

With the kids in bed, Brynn and I decide that now is a good time for us to get some sleep too. Just like every day lately, it seems, we're going to need all the energy we can get tomorrow.

··●··

The next morning, we pack the kids up and head out to the site. I had an email from the vice president waiting as soon as I woke up. He's already there making preparations.

Upon arriving at the coordinates, we find an area marked off for parking. We leave the car and start walking towards the only people around. On the way, I'm amazed at the color of the sand. "It definitely earns its name," I tell Brynn. It's a pure white like I've never seen in sand before. The ground is hard, but I can see dunes in the distance to our right. The mountains to the south and west make the scene even more beautiful.

When we get closer, I realize it's the vice president himself, sleeves rolled up and helping spread a barrier of police tape and cones. We jump in and help while the kids play.

"Everyone should be arriving shortly," he tells me. "I made a public announcement last night after our last call. There's no telling how many people will be here. Multiple news crews will be here as well, for the people across the world that can't make it." He points to a few structures in the distance. "Those are bathrooms and a water station. It'll be warm here today. I've made sure there is plenty of water for everyone."

"It looks like you've got everything covered," I tell him.

"We do. There are plenty of military members

around to help. We're getting a medical tent put together now, too. If you'd like, feel free to take your kids to play over on the dunes. We've got space up front saved for you, so you don't have to worry about beating the crowds."

"Thanks," I say. Brynn and I scoop up the kids and take them to play on the massive dunes, and I watch as the people start to arrive in droves.

After about an hour, we head back. The area is full of people now. Cars are parked for as far as the eye can see, in every direction.

We arrive at the front of the throng of people, finding Vice President Harwell quickly. We stand beside him, our waists against the line of police tape. I see now that there are coolers throughout the mass of people, too. Military members can be spotted carrying cases of water, keeping the coolers full so no one has to move if they don't want to.

Eleven fifty-five hits, and the group begins to silence. The sky is a beautiful cloudless blue today, which is perfect for an event such as this. Looking back, I see nothing but a sea of people. *It must be millions,* I think.

Looking to Brynn, I ask her, "Are you ready?"

"I've never been as ready for something in my entire life," she responds sincerely. "The last few weeks have been a wild ride."

"Yes, they have," I reply. "But I think the next fifty years are going to be crazier than you ever imagined."

"You're right. But it's a good crazy. I can't wait. To

experience something like this with you is amazing, Ira. I'm proud of you."

"Thanks, hun. I'm proud of you too. I couldn't have done any of it without your help." Lacing my fingers through hers, I look to the horizon.

I can hear it now. A deep, thrumming vibration. As it grows closer, I can feel it. I look up, and spot the black dot growing larger in the sky. The lower it gets, the more defined it is.

It appears more rectangular now, long and bulky, dropping smoothly from the sky. The size, although I expected it, is still a powerful sight.

The noise fills my ears, and I remember the earplugs I picked up on the way. I throw them in the kids' ears as the noise grows stronger. I hand a pair to Brynn and put mine in as well.

Just in time, it turns out. The level of noise is so powerful now, I see most people in the crowd placing hands over their ears. My bones vibrate with the ground, almost making my teeth chatter.

The ship is larger than I ever thought. It's well over half a mile in length, and its width isn't even discernible yet. It is at least two hundred feet tall too, and covered completely in gleaming black and grey metal.

As it nears the ground, the sound changes. It sounds like a fog horn from a massive naval vessel mixed with the sound of vibration. Everything around us shakes now, and car alarms begin to go off in the parking area. The ship, even at one mile away, has caused the wind to pick up, too. Sand and dirt blow freely after being forced from underneath the ship, peppering the crowd. I release Brynn's hand and grab a shoulder of each child in front of me.

Finally, with one final release of dust from underneath, a huge puff of air with the accompanying blast of vibration and sound, the massive craft touches Earth.

·24·
Zavilisk
White Sands, New Mexico

THE crowd stands in awe as the dust settles. I can hear the ship's engines cycling down, slowly getting quieter before shutting down completely. The silence that follows is unbelievable. I don't think there has been a single time in history where a crowd this size was so quiet. Not a single voice can be heard. The world, it seems, has lost its ability to speak.

Slowly, a large door, resembling that of a hanger bay, lowers itself to the ground at the rear of the ship. It creates a ramp, large enough to move massive pieces of equipment or amounts of people in and out with ease.

Unexpectedly, I hear a voice over my radio. "Ira?" Captain Alter asks.

"Yes, I'm here," I respond.

"It is safe to move forward. Please, only yourself, your family, and the leaders at this time. We have a system in place to provide tours, but we can only handle so many at once."

"Okay, we'll get a plan together here then make our way to you. You might want to consider sending someone here to help coordinate."

"They're already on the way," he replies.

"I'll be there soon!" I tell him excitedly.

The vice president has already begun gathering the world leaders, and an announcement begins to play over speakers, telling the crowd to please wait until the tours can begin.

Once everyone in our official party is together, we begin our walk. Brynn and I each hold two hands, and they are full of questions. It's difficult to explain to them what is going on, so we keep it simple by telling them we're going to meet some people that are visiting.

Getting closer to the ship, the increased clarity gives us a much better view. While the metal appears smooth, the facade is anything but. There are sensors and antennae everywhere, jutting off in every direction. Even more are concealed beneath the metal, creating bulges across the surface. There are also little scrapes dotting the surface, where small meteors must have scraped the ship as they passed by.

The bridge of the ship, where the cockpit and observation floors are, is small compared to the rest of the ship. I knew the other floors were larger, but I had no idea how much larger.

"This is the same ship you were on, correct?" Vice President Harwell asks.

"Yes," I tell him. "It is called the Zavilisk.

"It's enormous," Brynn adds. "No matter how well you described it, I never thought it would be this big."

"I honestly didn't know it was quite this big, myself," I tell her. "I didn't exactly see it from the outside."

"True," she laughs.

The closer we get, the more I notice. I can see the large thrusters now, visible at the front and back of the ship, with scorch marks showing the amount of heat they produce. There are also smaller ports visible that serve an unknown purpose. It surprises me that there are no wings. The ship must rely on sheer power to maintain stability.

As we aim our group for the open door at the rear of the ship, I see people walking toward us. Once they are close enough to see clearly, I realize it is Kalis, Alter, and Birkim. They meet us and introduce themselves to the world leaders.

"Ira!" Kalis says excitedly. "I'm so glad to see you again. I'm proud of you, my friend. We knew you could do it."

"I'm happy to see you too, Kalis. This is Brynn, my wife. And these are my kids," I say, pointing to everyone.

"It's so nice to finally meet you all. Before we spend too much time here talking, though, let us show you aboard."

Breaking us up into three groups, Brynn and I naturally stay with the kids, and the vice president is added into our group. Other people are added in as well, and our group is complete. With Kalis leading our group, we begin walking as he points out and describes different parts of the Zavilisk.

Turning a corner, we begin to walk up the ramp into the belly of the ship. It occurs to me that this is the first time I've ever walked aboard. Last time, I was transported here with no control. This time, I'm showing the rest of the world what the Zavilisk is like.

We continue walking, and Kalis never runs out of things inside to show us. We move deeper into the ship, traveling up and down staircases, the conversation never faltering.

Reaching the floor containing the engines, he takes more time to explain. We stop at two giant machines at the rear of the ship. They are each the size of a house, easily twenty feet wide by fifty feet long, and reaching a height of fifteen feet. The metal is light grey, with markings that must indicate names and technical information. Wires connect different pieces. "These are the nuclear reactors used to supply power to the engines," he tells us.

"*Those* are reactors?" vice president Harwell asks. "They're so small!"

"Yes, they are. Trust me, we will show you how

to downsize many pieces of technology you already use. We will also be able to increase their efficiency."

Above the reactors are two more machines. Though they aren't as big as the reactors, they are still large. They look like two large black boxes, but each has a tube that exits the rear wall of the ship.

"What are those?" Brynn asks, pointing to them.

"Those are the laser propulsion systems," Kalis replies.

"Laser propulsion systems?"

"They provide addition thrust, and faster direction changing. The special lasers compress all of the dark matter, causing it to explode when the lasers lose contact with it. This pushes the ship forward. By turning the laser arrays, the resulting explosions help turn the ship."

"This is amazing," Brynn responds. "So many things we have never even thought of on Earth."

"There is plenty more, too," he says. "Follow me." We do as asked, and eventually find ourselves standing in front of two giant tanks. They are tubular and have no seams that I can see. The only thing that breaks the smooth shape is a connection at the top of each with a large hose leading from it.

"These hold the air we use to maintain our location when the ship is still. Whether that means orbiting, or just staying stationary in space, we use this," he says, patting one of the tanks. "There are hoses throughout the exterior walls of the ship, taking oxygen to various ports. These ports each have a nozzle that can be aimed in specific directions. With a burst of air, they control rotation and motion when the main engines are on standby. Nozzles under the ship also aid us in providing a smooth landing."

"How does the ship have enough air for all of that, and still save enough for you to breath?" the vice president asks.

"Oxygen is produced here on the ship," Kalis explains. "But don't ask me how it works. It is another technology that only one species has mastered. They provide the equipment for use on our ships. While I am trained in usage, routine maintenance, and small repairs, I do not know exactly how the machine creates oxygen."

"Is there a lot of technology like that? Proprietary?"

"There are plenty of pieces of technology that many understand, yes. But we wouldn't call it proprietary. While only one species may be able to create something, that's not locked in. If you were able to take any machine here apart and understand how it works, you are free to recreate it. It just rarely happens with some of these."

We begin walking again, heading up one of the great spiral staircases while people in our group continue to ask questions. Reaching the top, we make a left into another large room. This room, though, contains nothing but one enormous machine that nearly fills the room completely. It spreads from wall to wall, nearly twenty feet in width. The shiny black surface reflecting the light around us, making it seem even larger. The machine is spherical, but the entire surface is covered in sensors and hoses. On the side facing the door, there is a large holographic screen with a keyboard mounted below it.

"This," Kalis begins, "is the matter distributer. "This is what we use to move people onto the ship. It is also used to move the ship from one point in space to another, allowing us to move great distances instantly. As its name suggests, it reorganizes dark matter into a tunnel. A doorway, of sorts. On one side sits us, the ship. On the other is the location that we want to go. The ship is then shifted through, instantly appearing at the coordinates we programmed in. It works the same way with people. From our isolation room, they can be moved wherever the coordinates designate.

"It takes enormous amounts of power for this machine to move an entire ship. The nuclear reactor that is dedicated to operating this has enough fuel for about ten universal shifts. Moving a person takes considerably less."

"How do you make sure someone doesn't end up floating in space after being sent to incorrect coordinates?" someone in the group asks.

"Oh, there are plenty of failsafes in place. The system recognizes the difference between coordinates in space and those on land. When preparing to shift a person, information like their species and equipment they have with them is required to be entered to complete the process, ensuring that a species that breathes oxygen isn't sent to a planet with nothing but nitrogen to breathe. It is a very safe process."

"What happens if you run out of fuel?" someone else asks.

"It takes a long, long time to get home," Kalis replies. "Kidding! There is a reserve unit, somewhat like a large capacitor, that holds enough energy for one shift. This unit is preprogrammed with the ship's home port, to ensure that it makes it back to where it belongs and can be refueled."

We continue walking, and the members of our group fill the halls with conversation. They talk about everything from the size of the ship to the amazing lighting system, everyone in awe of the level of technology here. I fill Brynn in on other little things that I hadn't told her about the ship.

Arriving one floor up and in another large room, we find ourselves standing in front of another large black box. It appears solid, but I'm sure it's not. The metal is dull, and the box hums as we get near it. There is only one group of wires leading away from it, and they go directly into the wall.

"This is the gravity equalizer," Kalis tells us. "It provides the ship with gravity when we are in an environment with none, like space. Also, we can adjust it to equal the gravity of the planet we intend to land on, allowing us some time to adjust to the difference. This function helps quite a bit. Smaller ships do not have this function, so it can be a shock moving from the gravity of the ship to that of whatever planet they arrive on."

As we walk some more, it is obvious people are becoming more relaxed. The questions come easier, and Kalis struggles to answer each of them before the next one comes. The tour has now reached areas of the ship that I am familiar with. I show my family the room I stayed in, surprising Brynn with its size and simplicity.

On the way to the viewing room, Kalis explains the technologies found in the cockpit. All are understood fairly quickly, as they relate to our naval and air technologies.

"The radar system," he adds, "is unique in comparison to what you currently have. It connects to other nearby systems. If there are any other ships nearby, or other planets in the galaxy with radar systems, it casts a huge net. You can see any obstacles from great distances away, leaving you plenty of time to navigate around them. There are also accident avoidance systems and alarms."

When we reach the viewing room, the sidebar conversations and questions cease. Everyone remembers what I described, and they are eager to get to the windows and see the view that I had, regardless of whether there are stars outside or desert. They stare in awe, now whispering quietly to each other, some obviously trying to picture the view that I had.

"It's amazing to see, just like this," Brynn says. "I can't even imagine what it was like for you in space."

"Well, I hope that one day you won't have to imagine it," I tell her. "Hopefully, one day you can join me, standing in front of a window just like this."

"I'll keep my fingers crossed," Brynn replies playfully.

"How does this ship compare in size to other ships?" someone asks Kalis.

"This ship is average in just about every way. Its size, while massive to you, is definitely not the biggest. There are others that dwarf this. Some are the size of some of your large cities. Technology wise, this is an old ship. There are plenty that are older, as well. There are also many ships that are newer, with much newer technology. Reactors that require even less fuel, for example."

"Wow. I can't imagine ships larger than this," Vice President Harwell says. "I don't know what to say. All of this is a lot to take in."

"I understand that it is a lot," Kalis replies. "A decision is not necessary today. You have as much time as you'd like."

"No, no, that's not what I meant. I can only speak directly for myself, but I know from the conversations I've heard and been involved in, the general consensus is that we want in. I know we'll need to make a formal announcement. Really, I just meant I feel like I could see it all five times and still never really grasp it all."

Kalis laughs. "I understand! It took our friend Ira here a while to fully grasp everything as well. He was well into his time back on Earth before he fully understood what was happening."

"He's right," I say. "Don't feel bad for being a

little confused or feeling insignificant. That's definitely how I felt for days," I tell the crowd.

I hear murmurs of agreement, the people gathered here sounding relieved to not be alone in their thoughts. *Try realizing you are the only one that can do what I've done,* I think. *Then you'd really feel lost.*

"After seeing all of this, what is the next step?" Vice President Harwell asks. "What happens after we decide to accept? Hypothetically, of course."

"Well," Kalis begins, "once you accept our help, and the council accepts your plans to manage your planet, we would bring you the material to build a ship. We also provide workers and expert assistance for this. We would also give you devices to use for communicating with us, and anything else you might need. We would station people here to assist your scientists in learning, and help them in their efforts to create some of the advanced technologies we've shown you. Once you are capable, they will leave. We would also provide you with maps and coordinates. The coordinates would show every advanced planet, every planet used for mining resources, and planets that you have to stay away from."

"Planets we have to stay away from?" someone asks, concerned.

"Yes. But not because there is any risk to us. Because there would be a risk to them. We do not want to prematurely contact a species that is not prepared. It can greatly hurt our cause."

"Aah, that makes sense," says the vice president.

With no more immediate questions, we begin the long walk back to the outside world. On the way, we only pass one other group touring the ship, making me wonder how many people will be able to make it in today. I have a feeling the people outside will wait outside however long is necessary for them to see the inside of the ship and its amazing technology.

Once we reach the ramp, Kalis stops the group one last time. "When you are ready, we will need a formal acceptance of our assistance. Also, we will need to bring you to the cockpit to have a video conference with the council. There, you will submit to them your plan, and they will either accept or deny. You already know what happens after that. Take your time. Ira will let me know when you are ready. Are there any more questions?"

No one asks anything else, and we begin the walk back to the parking area. It eases my stress just a little to know that this hurdle has been crossed. There is only one left, and it is the most important of all. *I just hope the plan they came up with is functional,* I think. *We're almost there.*

· 25 ·
Pressure
White Sands, New Mexico

WE get about half way between the ship and the parking area when the vice president stops us. He pulls our entire group in close, so we can all hear each other.

"Wait here a minute," he says, turning from us and pulling out his cell phone.

"I wonder what that's about," says Brynn, eying me sideways.

"I really don't know," I reply, watching him. He ends the call and walks back over to us.

"Let's head back to the ship. We're going to meet the other two groups of world leaders. Might as well be efficient, right?"

I don't ask what he means. *How is walking back*

as one large group any more efficient than walking back as three separate smaller groups?

Brynn looks to me and mouths "What?"

I shake my head, just as clueless a she is. We start walking back, and the ship is still an amazing sight. The sun is behind it now, causing it to appear as if it has an aura, since the light is appearing from every side, like a corona. The white sand adds to the effect. It reminds me of the interior of the ship, with light emanating from nowhere and everywhere at once.

"It's beautiful," Brynn says, reading my mind.

"It is. Hopefully, we'll be able to see it plenty more."

We make it to the rear of the ship again, and the other two groups are now there waiting on us. We stand there, on the lowered rear door, while everyone intermingles. The conversations floating around me seem positive, with not a single negative comment reaching my ears. All I can hear is praise.

"Can we have a minute?" Vice President Harwell asks, looking at Kalis. "We'd really like to talk in private for a bit."

"Of course, of course. Take your time. I'll be back in a few minutes if you need anything," he replies, walking away.

Once the room is empty of everyone but humans, the vice president calls me over. I still can't figure out why we're waiting here instead of walking back across the desert. It's getting dark.

"Ira," he begins. "We are ready. My phone call

outside was quick because we are all in agreement. We want to submit our plan to the council."

"What? How?" I ask. "You don't have the opinions of the scientists yet. Or the psychologists. You can't be ready."

"We do have their opinions. Look right over there," he says, pointing. I glance to my right, and sure enough, the four I invited are standing there, gaggled together with what must be more from other countries. "They've been mixed in with the other groups throughout the evening. They didn't get quite as intensive of a tour as we did, but they all still agree. We are ready."

"You have the plan with you?"

"We do," he says, giving me an odd smile.

"Well, where is it? I was expecting something written. It would have to be a lot, I figured you all had made up a binder or document or something."

Putting his hand on my shoulder, he squares himself to me and looks me in the eye. "We have it right here," he says, patting my shoulder.

"Wait, you mean my plan? Are you serious?"

"Very serious, Ira. The others and I talked all night last night. We couldn't come up with a single thing that was any better than what you said in Geneva. So we want you to present it again. Exactly the same as before. Lay out the problems, and then outline the possible solutions."

"I guess I can do that," I respond, amazed. Never would I have imagined that my plan was the best possibility.

"Remember, it doesn't have to be exact. It just needs to be laid out in a manner that is easy for them to understand. They just need to be able to see your vision. If they can, then we're in the clear."

"Thanks. No pressure, huh?" I say, only half joking.

"No, Ira. Not really. We know you can do it. It was your idea, after all."

Kalis walks back into the room, and I suddenly become very nervous. I glance to the vice president, and he nods towards Kalis. *I guess there's no point in hesitating.*

I meet Kalis at the top of the ramp. "Hello, my friend," he says. "Is there something you need?"

"Yes," I tell him anxiously. I pause, gathering my wits, before finishing. "I need you to take me to the cockpit."

"Why the cockpit?"

"Because I need to present our plan to the council," I tell him.

"What?!" he exclaims loudly. "You are ready? I was not expecting an answer for a couple of days."

"Well, as the vice president says," I start, remembering his comment before we began walking, "We might as well be efficient."

"Okay. If you are prepared, then I suppose you may follow me. They stay on standby once a research vessel lands, so that they may be contacted at any time."

"Let me run and talk to Brynn. I'll be right back."

"Sure!" he replies. "I'll be right here waiting."

Turning, I walk back down to the base of the ramp. Brynn's eyes meet mine, and I can tell she is wondering what is going on.

"I don't even know where to begin," I tell her. "The world leaders are ready. The scientists and psychologists are as well. They've decided already. They want to do it."

"That's great news!" Brynn responds excitedly. Her smile can't seem to get any bigger. "When do they submit their plan?"

"That's the thing. They aren't going to. They don't have a plan. They have mine, and I'm going to submit it to the council."

"My God, Ira. I was not expecting that."

"I wasn't either. The vice president just voluntold me. I'll be back soon. I'll see if Kalis or Alter will bring you guys up to the lounge in the viewing room so that you can relax. I'll be in the cockpit for a bit."

"That's fine. Good luck, Ira," Brynn says, just as supportive as always. "I love you."

"I love you to Brynn," I reply, turning and heading back up the ramp. *Well, this is it,* I think as I meet Kalis at the top. We begin walking, and my nerves are shot. The biggest moment in the history of Earth, and I'm the one that's supposed to make it work. *No pressure at all.*

··●··

Kalis and I are both relatively silent as we walk back to the folded down hangar door. I can't seem to form any words, after the event that just took place. The conversation with the council keeps replaying through my head, blocking anything else from getting in.

"Your family is already there, waiting for you," he tells me. "Everyone is else still there waiting as well."

"Thanks," I respond, not sure what else to say. My brain is still only semi-functional. I can barely even think. Trying to focus, I look at the walls as we pass. I'm still trying to find inconsistencies that aren't there. Only perfection exists on this ship. Running my hand against one, the smoothness helps to calm me.

"The council wants to meet you," Kalis suddenly tells me.

"What? Meet me? They just did," I respond. "When did they tell you that?"

"No, Ira," Kalis says. "They want to meet you in person. They told me after you left the room."

"Why in person?" I ask. "Is that normal?"

"No, it isn't. I've never seen them request to meet like that. I don't know what it is for. It could be anything."

"Weird. Okay. Well, I'm sure we can work it out. If they want to meet in person, I don't have a problem with that."

We fall back into silence as we descend the last spiral staircase. Approaching the end of the ship, I see everyone still loitering on the ramp, waiting for whatever news I bring. Brynn approaches first, with the kids. She has a smile even bigger than last time. *How is that possible?*

"How'd it go?" she asks.

"Please, wait. I need to tell everyone at the same time."

"Okay. I think they're all ready," Brynn tells me, squeezing my hand.

I stop at the top of the ramp, and everyone gathers around. They come in close, eager to hear me speak. There's even a TV crew here now, ready to document the moment. I can't come up with a way to get the words out without a flood of emotion following them. I'm starting to recognize more of them now, which doesn't help. I can easily pick out Vice President Harwell. I see my scientist friends standing off to the side as well. France and Geneva are up front, the anxiety on their faces apparent.

Knowing these people personally makes this even harder to do. I never imagined how difficult it would be to deliver this message. The emotions welling up in my chest make me feel like I'm drowning. I know they're going to burst out as soon as I begin talking to the crowd.

I look to Brynn and the kids, and they put me at ease. Seeing those smiling face, filled with love, seems to be able to make everything better.

Finally, after the awkward silence that my presence caused has filled everyone with nervousness, the vice president speaks.

"Well? What did they say? How did it go? What's the next step, Ira?"

I pause before answering, trying to meet eyes with every person in the crowd. Taking a deep breath, I manage to break my silence. "How long do you think it'll take to gather enough people to begin production? Because this," I say, waving my arm towards the ship, "is here to stay. Welcome to the community."

Once the words leave my lips, I can't hold it back anymore. I collapse to the edge of the floor where it joins the ramp, and finally release the tears of joy I've been holding in. *It's finally done. The future is here.*

· 26 ·
All Aboard
White Sands, New Mexico

THE last two months have been a blur. In the beginning, I was paraded. Every news agency aired videos of me. First the video of Geneva, then the video of me telling the world leaders the news on the lowered ramp of the ship. After the videos had dried up, I was interviewed. I've done so many interviews now, I feel like I could have been a public relations representative if I had wanted. I finally had to stop. I'd rather spend time with my family.

We have been back and forth from home to New Mexico fairly regularly. Almost every other week, we have come to the Zavilisk, to see Kalis or to help with something. The kids love being here, too. The ship is an endless jungle gym to them.

Construction has begun on Earth's first deep space ship as well. It is nearly identical to the Zavilisk, but with newer equipment. The feat of engineering is currently being built right beside the Zavilisk. This made it much easier for us to work with the other people who have come to assist.

Supply ships began showing up almost immediately. Within a week, we started receiving huge shipments of metal from some other planet, deep within the universe.

The carriers that brought it were absolutely enormous. They resemble aircraft carriers, but instead of planes they haul materials. There is a high bridge, similar to the Zavilisk. This bridge sits high on a mast, which stands even taller above the deck. Large containers are attached to the deck of the ships, which then transport them throughout the universe.

The most amazing feature of these ships, though, is what they do when they land. Instead of sitting high above the ground, they burrow. Giant grinders protrude from the sides of the carrier after landing. Once they begin spinning, they churn up and displace every bit of dirt and rock around them, slowly dropping the ship into the Earth. Once the deck is level with the ground around it, the grinders stop, and vehicles are able to drive directly onto the deck to unload the cargo.

Wes particularly loved seeing this. Unfortunately, he was only able to see it twice. Two of the carriers landed first, and afterward each new carrier just landed in the spot already dug out. I'm just proud to see him taking an interest in it. *He could be a great Captain one day,* I think.

The most amazing sight of all, though, is the action being taken to make the world a better place. When the council heard my ideas for helping Earth get back to where it should be, they immediately accepted the plan and offered to help in any way possible. They loved my resourcefulness in using products that weren't even available to us yet to fix what is currently wrong with Earth.

Almost every bit of technology used has been upgraded. Nuclear power has gotten much safer. Coal is nonexistent. Gasoline is only being used until there are enough electric and nuclear-powered vehicles for everyone to have one.

Pollution has already decreased immensely. Just through education, a lot of it was eliminated quickly. Once people realized that there were better ways to eliminate waste, like recycling or burning, most littering stopped. Plastic is slowly being phased out completely, replaced by metal that is ever present throughout the universe. Operations are underway in every ocean and sea to round up the rest of the floating trash. Siphons have been installed along the coasts, along with floating vessels that suck up all inorganic matter.

Famine has ended already. On top of everyone coming together and sharing the food that is produced, the council had ships sent with almost limitless amounts of food, to help us get on the right track. Now, everyone eats, and no one is hungry. As an interesting byproduct in all of this is, everyone eats healthier as well. The rate of obesity and general unhealthiness has plummeted.

Numerous countries have dropped their borders now, too. Europe is now officially known only as Europe. There are no individual countries anymore. France and Germany led the way, with everyone else following them soon after. North and South Korea reunited. The walls around the United States began to come down the day after my announcement. Citizens and government contractors alike were out in droves, tearing them down brick by brick. These bricks and cinderblocks were then used to build housing around the area used for ship building, to provide all of the workers and their family a place to live.

War has ceased to exist. Everyone is focused on the goals common to all, like space travel and incorporating new technology into everyday life. All countries have discontinued defense spending, and used that funding for other things. Pilots are being retrained on the new flying vehicles available to us. Soldiers are being trained in science, and will eventually become the men and women who are the first to discover and walk on new planets.

All nuclear material has been removed from weapons and converted into fuel for ships. The metal from missiles and guns alike was melted down to be used elsewhere. The only weapons that still exist are those used for hunting.

The planet is healing itself faster than anyone thought it would. The holes in the ozone layer are already smaller than they were, and will eventually close. The atmosphere itself will become healthier, with no harmful chemicals floating through it any longer. Water temperatures are predicted to regulate themselves, and ice shelves will grow back to the size they were one hundred years ago. Climatologists say that freak storms will stop happening, and weather across the Earth will normalize quickly. All of this will make food easier to produce, eventually eliminating our small reliance on food from outside sources.

With common goals bringing people together, everyone is generally happier. Just as I predicted, racism and sexism are gone. How can color matter when there is a universe full of other species out there? And with war gone, people are now traveling more, able to see and experience things they never would have dreamed of before.

Money is not used anymore, either. There is no need for it when everyone understands their role in the brave new world. Not relying on money also contributes to a better overall mood. Someone that lived on the street eight months ago can now travel freely to Sydney, Australia if he wanted, and it wouldn't cost him a dime.

Being able to experience all of this has brought Brynn and I even closer together than we were before. It also made me forget about the meeting I was supposed to have with the council. That is, until Kalis decided to remind me today.

"Yes, Kalis, I remember," I tell him. *I do remember, now that you just said something about it.* "When should we go?"

"Whenever you are ready. We will leave plenty of people here to help with construction on your ship, of course. And it will only take a day or two before we are back. Your family is welcome to come as well."

With his last sentence, my face lights up. "I can bring my kids and Brynn?"

"Of course, my friend. Why not? You should remove yourself from this mindset that only the elite or select few get to enjoy space travel. Anyone can go anywhere now, my friend."

"I know, I know," I tell him. "It's still a hard idea to wrap my brain around."

"You will get there. So, you are ready to go then?"

"Yes, Kalis. We can go. Let me tell Brynn and the kids first, though. I don't want to surprise them by bringing them aboard and then just lifting off."

"No problem," Kalis tells me. "We're ready when you are. We'll be waiting in the cockpit."

I make my way back to Brynn, and surprise her with the news.

"We're going to visit the council," I tell her.

"We?!" she asks excitedly. "We're about to travel through space?!"

"Yes, we are," I laugh. "Are you ready? It'll just be a day. The kids are coming too."

"Of course, I'm ready! How could I say no to something like that?"

"Good! We can stay in the cockpit for the flight." Turning to the kids, I say, "All aboard!"

They laugh as they run up the ramp, excited to embark on their first real journey. Brynn looks just as excited, chasing them to the staircase that will lead them to the cockpit.

I turn and give Earth one last look, before making my way up to the spiral stairs.

By the time I make it to the cockpit, the ramp has already closed and the engines are ready. Brynn and the kids have taken up seats facing the window, ready to enjoy the view. I greet Alter and tell him we're ready to go.

Looking out the window, I see the ground slowly fall away from the ship. I can't even feel the ship move. The only indication is the Earth growing smaller. Soon enough, we are in space, hovering high about the planet I call home.

"Are you ready for your first shift through space?" Alter asks.

"As ready as I'm gonna get," I tell him.

"It's not bad. You won't feel a thing."

"If you say so. I've felt it every other time," I retort.

"You'll see," Kalis cuts in. "Trust us. Ready?"

"Just do it!"

Alter pushes a button, and the scene outside the giant windows changes instantly, like changing the channel on a TV. Instead of the darkness of space, we now see a hulking metal structure hovering in front of us. Below, I can faintly see a small planet.

"That was it?" I ask.

"That was it," Alter says. "I told you, it wouldn't be bad."

"Wow. I really didn't feel a thing. What is that in front of us?"

"That is where the council meets. We're going to dock there so that they can board the ship," Kalis tells me.

"Oh, okay. I assumed we'd land on a planet somewhere."

"Well, there is a planet below us. But the council stays up here in this orbital station. They prefer to stay away from the distractions of everyday life while performing their duties."

"That makes sense," I say as I feel a slight tap from the ship making contact with the station.

"We're here," he says. "In just a minute, a door on the side of the ship will open so that they may pass through. They'll be here shortly."

There's little talk while we wait. I'm too nervous to say much, and Brynn appears the same. The kids are running wild, without a care in the world. Other members of the ship have no problem playing with them, helping us keep them occupied.

Finally, I see a congregation begin to form, new people filing through the doorway from the stairwell. They all appear relatively human, minus a few differences here and there. Skin color, shapes of appendages like ears and fingers, and height are the only real differences.

When they arrive in front of me, the first person speaks.

"Hello, Ira. I am Ledoran. I'm glad to finally meet you in person." His voice is deep and gravelly, the opposite of what I was expecting, considering his light frame.

"Hello," I reply. "It's nice to meet you too. This is my wife, Brynn," I say, gesturing to her. Pointing across the room, I add, "Those four savages running around the room are my kids."

"It is nice to meet you as well, Brynn." Turning back to me, he says, "We wanted to meet you today so that we may talk with you about your quest. We'd also like to hear, from your perspective, how progress is coming on Earth."

"No problem," I say. I tell them how everything went, and the problems we faced getting to this point. They are surprised to hear that a person in a position of power had to be removed. "He was the only person in the world that was standing in the way. It had to be done," I say.

"And what do you think about the progress now?" Ledoran asks.

"It's amazing. I never imagined something like this would happen so fast. The ship is nearly done. We have successfully integrated much of the technology brought to us. Earth is already much cleaner and safer than it was before. I suppose we should be thanking you for that."

"You do not need to thank us," he says. "It was your people that came together and made everything happen so fast. We just provided a reason to do it."

"Well thank you for the reason," I tell them. "The people of Earth have a new path to follow now, and we're already doing well with it. I can only imagine the fantastic things we can do along the way."

"The rest of the universe has a lot to learn from you humans. We're happy to have you join us. We're all going to be better off with your people in the universal community with us.

"This brings me to the last reason we asked you to come here. I understand that Kalis gave you a gift before departing the Zavilisk the first time?"

"He did. It's beautiful."

"Well, I don't want him to think we are attempting to outdo him, but we would like to present a gift to you as well. It is our token of gratitude for everything you have done. As I said before, the universe will be a better place now. And we appreciate all of the effort and strife you went through to make it to this point."

"Thank you," I say, not knowing what to expect.

"If you'll look out this window," he says, pointing to one on the side of the ship, "you will see the gift we would like for you to accept."

I look out, not seeing anything that he would be talking about. "All I see is the orbital station and another ship docked on the other side."

"Exactly," he tells me. "I hope you enjoy your new ship. Feel free to name it whatever you like. It is yours to use as you see fit."

"A ship?!" I shout. "You're giving me a ship of my own?!"

"We are indeed," Ledoran replies. "Captain Alter will assist you on your trip home. By the time you arrive back on Earth, you should be proficient in its operation. Also, should you ever choose a different path, we would welcome your addition to the council. Your insight has proven to be invaluable."

"Thank you," I tell him. "Really. There aren't words I can use to make you understand how thankful I am."

"We are sure that you will do great things, Ira. Your family as well. Take care, my friend. We hope to see you soon."

With that, he turns to leave. The other members of the council follow, and they disappear through the doorway. *If I didn't know better, I'd say I dreamed all of this.*

Brynn walks over, lacing her fingers between mine. We stand there, silent, looking at our new ship. It waits, gleaming. The beautiful metal is shining at us, begging us to take it for its inaugural flight. "That's ours?" she asks.

"All ours," I tell her as I shift my eyes to the black space beyond. The final frontier, and it's mine to explore. I never imagined I'd see this day, or anything close to it. But it's here, nonetheless. "Ready for a new beginning? There's a whole new life here for us, if you'll join me."

"There's nothing I'd rather do," she says, kissing me. I can't imagine a better life for the kids, either."

"I had always hoped they would be as interested in space as I was. Looks like they don't have a choice," I say, smiling. "And we've always got our home on Earth to go back to whenever we feel like it."

Earth is safer than it has been in years. Its inhabitants will continue to thrive for millions more, one people in a universe full of life. That alone is more than I could have ever asked for.

I will *do great things with this ship,* I tell myself. I have no choice. After helping everyone on Earth reach a new level, I'm confident I can assist others in doing the same. There's another Ira out there, somewhere. He's staring up at the sky just like I did, full of hope and awe. I'm going to find him.

Per Aspera, Ad Astra.
"Through hardships, to the stars."
—Motto of NASA

Epilogue

Vlastick Galaxy, Lynx Arc Supercluster, 2019

MY ship has been a dream. It's fast. Unbelievably fast. Sometimes, I still find myself struggling to get used to it. We were surprised at how easy it is to operate. Its enormous size leads the mind to inaccurate conclusions. It is, however, more than just Brynn and I can handle ourselves. I found people on Earth who were good candidates to help, and we spent all of our first year speeding through the universe. There is nowhere that we cannot go.

The name I chose is 'Ima Profundi.' It's Latin, and translates to 'Deepest of the Deep.' I thought it was fitting, since aboard this ship are the first humans to ever travel into deep space.

I decided immediately that I wanted to operate it as a research vessel, like the Zavilisk. The council approved my decision as fast as I made it. They have always believed that I was destined for great things. Their belief has started wearing off on me.

Hovering just outside of the Vlastick Galaxy, I decide to check everything one more time. Skimming the pages, I look for anything that might stick out. If there are too many negatives, the council may decide to change their mind. I don't want that to happen on my first contact.

My analysts have done an incredible job. They have logged and verified absolutely everything about this species. Languages, cultures, financials, anything that could even possibly be considered important has been documented. As far as I can see, they are a good candidate. Nothing looks out of the ordinary. My list of rules has been met, so it should go well. I think we're ready.

"Brynn, have we got a good landing zone selected?"

"Yeah, I just finalized the report. We've got three decent options. All are in the desert regions. One is on the planet's most populous landmass."

"Okay, we'll go with that last one. Select coordinates that are as close to a population zone as we can safely get. I don't want them to have to travel a thousand miles from the nearest city just to get to us."

"Sounds good. I'll get those coordinates uploaded now."

"Great. Thanks, hun."

"Simon, how are your models?"

"It's pretty rough, Ira. You already know that their star is failing. The galaxies in this area are old, and the stars are even older. They're all going to be gone relatively soon, in universal time. This planet is already losing much of its atmosphere due to heat. Its foliage is dying off, and animals are going extinct. They really don't have much time left."

"Well, we're getting here just in time then, huh?" I reply.

I chose this area for a reason. I want to help species that not only are getting close to our level of advancement, but are also close to destruction. I didn't decide this for a challenge. I want to help these people because their planet could be the reason they don't make it, not themselves.

This doesn't sit right with me. These people have been relatively kind to their planet. Surely a lot less destructive than we were to Earth. They are a fairly calm people as well. There is little war here, and no discrimination to speak of. I don't want the universe to lose a species that has done all the right things since the beginning. If I can change that, I will.

Fortunately, the council agrees with me. While they aren't as advanced as the council prefers, they understand that the time constraints override some of their standards.

The kids run up behind my chair, and I turn to catch them before they're gone again.

"Hey, guys! I need to talk to you for a second," I tell them. "You know when we land, you have to stay here, right? You won't be able to go out onto their planet until we're sure it's safe. And they need to grow accustomed to us before we start bringing our children around."

I get nods in return, accentuated by pouted lips. They're obviously not happy.

"Maybe once we've been here a few days, we'll find some children for you to play with. Just give it time."

Frowns transform into smiles, and they're off again. *Kids.*

"Hey Brynn, got those coordinates uploaded?" I ask.

"All done. I just checked the feed as well. The landing zone is clear."

"Thanks! You guys ready?"

I get a unanimous 'yes,' and turn back to my console. "I'm gonna shift us to just outside of their atmosphere, directly above the landing zone coordinates," I tell them. "We'll descend from there."

"Sounds good," replies Brynn. "Are you ready?"

"As ready as I'm gonna get. The only experience I have is what we went through on Earth. Hopefully, this goes better. I don't think overthrown rulers should be the norm."

"Ha, I hope that's not the case," Brynn says, smiling. "Let's do this."

"Alright," I say, flipping the cover from the button that controls the matter distributer. "Here we go!"

I mash the button down, and the view outside

of the window instantly changes. Instead of the blackness of space, I now see the horizon of a planet. It's larger than Earth, and nearly seventy-five percent water. This water, though, is nearly boiling.

The sun is behind the planet, throwing the landing zone into darkness. The parts that I can see are currently covered in clouds. We descend slowly, trying to be as quiet as possible. The engines on the Ima Profundi are loud when operating at full power, and the last thing I want to do is terrify these people. It'll already be scary, seeing a giant, shiny black ship descending to their world, so I'd rather not make it worse.

We break free of the cloud cover, and I pull our speed back even more. Not for stealth this time, but to enjoy the view. This is our first contact. We are the first in the universal community to ever come close to this planet. It's a pivotal moment for everyone involved, but even more so for those of us from Earth.

Brynn climbs up to the platform and stands beside me. We look out at the landscape before us, the ground only a few hundred feet below. From here, it still looks much like Earth. Once we land, though, that will change. No two planets are exactly alike. Even though the sky is dark, I can make out mountains in the distance. As Earthlike as it is, it's still an amazing sight.

The landing gear drops, signaled by the hydraulic sound of many posts sliding from the bottom of the ship. At the base of these, large sheets of metal extend and level themselves off with the landscape below us, prepared to hold the weight of the ship. I feel them touch as we land, compressing into themselves to alleviate the sudden change in pressure. The ship comes to a rest, and I immediately cycle down the engines, cutting power to everything but critical services. *We just became aliens.*

"Simon, what's the exterior temperature?"

"It's about ninety-two degrees right now. When their sun breaches the horizon, this will increase significantly."

"What about the gravity? Did we match it close enough?"

"Yes sir, we are at almost exactly the same gravity as the planet. We won't have any problems when we exit."

"And their atmospheric composition is as we expected?"

"It is. We won't need any supplemental oxygen. We may tire easily, as their oxygen content is a bit lower than ours, but we won't suffer any ill effects otherwise."

"Great, thanks," I say. "Brynn, you're certain that our translation modules were correct?"

"Yes. The analysts are confident in their work. We won't face any difficulty communicating."

"Alright, I guess that's it," I say, spinning away from my console and stepping to the floor. Brynn joins me, and we walk over to Simon's station.

"You guys ready?" I ask as we all head to the

door.

"I am," Simon responds. "This is an amazing moment."

"Yes, it is, Simon," I say. *Yes, it is.*

"What about you, Brynn?"

"I'm excited!" she says, happy as ever. She laces her fingers in mine as we make our last few steps to the airlock.

Here I stand, with only two doors between myself and a new planet. A planet that is much like Earth was three years ago. Oblivious to the workings of the universe. Oblivious to how close their planet is to failing, and how close they are to disappearing along with it. *I won't allow that to happen.*

While the past three years have been unexpected and exciting, I feel like this is the real start of our journey. Opening the outer airlock, we step through. Just as expected, the door closes automatically behind us. *This is it.*

I swipe my hand across the wall panel, and the outer airlock door opens before us. I pause for a second, taking in the new landscape. The lights in the distance indicate a city, and I assume someone will be here soon. I look first to Brynn, and then to Simon, and get slight nods from each of them.

"Here goes nothing," I say as I take my first tentative step.

Fact or Fiction?

The information provided was as accurate as I could make it while still maintaining the storyline. I'm going to try to explain what is real and what is not, and why I chose to use the information in the way that I did.

The characters themselves are mostly figments of my imagination. Some are based on my life while the rest I made up to further my story. I'll never tell which is which.

Most of the locations are real, though I took liberties in describing them all.

- Charlottesville, Virginia is a real city, and its distance from Washington DC is mostly accurate.
- Los Alamos, New Mexico is real and still exists today, and they really did conduct research there for the first nuclear bomb.
- CERN is real, and it sits on the border between France and Switzlerland.

- The Palexpo is, in fact, a convention center in Geneva, Switzerland. The interior, however, was my design.
- White Sands is the location of the first nuclear test, the Trinity test, and there is a monument there for you to check out in your spare time. The sand really is white.
- The Shapley Supercluster and Lynx Arc Superclusters are real too. The galaxies I named within, however, were made to suit my needs.

Space! Let me explain some of the concepts I wrote about. This stuff fascinates me, and if you made it this far, hopefully it does you too.

Superclusters are real. There are tons of them, filling the universe. They are made up of local groups, which are groups of galaxies. Not just five galaxies, either. Thousands. To make you feel even smaller, you should know that there are four hundred billion stars just in the Milky Way galaxy alone. And it's a small galaxy, compared to others. For more amazing space information, check out this article I wrote on my blog:

https://mycrazyopinion28.wordpress.com/2016/03/19/still-think-theres-no-other-life-in-the-universe-2/

There, you'll find a bunch of fun facts, and some conjecture on my part. I promise, once you're done you'll feel smaller than a grain of sand. I can't put it all here without turning this into a non-fiction chapter at the end of a fiction book. Please, do your own research as well. There is a lot of amazing information out there.

Do I know for a fact that there is other life out there? No. Do I believe there is? I sure do. I think you'd be crazy not to. Even a single-celled organism is life, after all.

About the Author

First of all, thank you for reading! This book is self-published, so I get to write about myself. If you're interested in writing, you should know that this is the hardest part of all. I'm just me. Let me try to dig up some facts and make it coherent.

I just decided to start writing again. I've always enjoyed it, but I have never attempted a novel until now. As far as my profession is concerned, I've done a lot of things in my life. Currently, I'm a Staff Sergeant in the US Army, and I love what I do.

When I'm not writing, working, or doing Army stuff, I enjoy fishing. Woodworking is another passion of mine, and I'm getting better with everything I make. I know it's not for everyone, but if you'd like to try, it is the best way I've found to de-stress after a long week. There's nothing like building something with your bare hands.

I have a three-year-old son and a one-year-old daughter, and I love each of them with every ounce of my being. If you're a parent, you know what I mean.

If you're not a parent, the day you figure out what I'm talking about will be the best day of your life.

Now, I have to ask a favor from all of you. The only way for me to become a better writer is with your help. Please, leave me a review wherever you purchased this. It'll only take a minute of your time, and it will benefit me immensely.

Thank you again for reading. I sincerely hope you enjoyed it. Also, since you've read this far, I want you to know: this is not the end of Ira Sanders.

Please feel free to contact me! You're welcome to ask questions, give me tips or criticism, or just start a chat.

Facebook:
https://www.facebook.com/BryanWritesBooks/

Blog:
https://mycrazyopinion28.wordpress.com/

Email:
bryanwritesbooks@gmail.com